Very Different

Very Different

and other stories

Anne Fine

mammoth

This collection first published in Great Britain 2001
by Mammoth, an imprint of Egmont Books UK
a division of Egmont Holding Limited
239 Kensington High Street, London W8 6SA

ISBN 0 7497 4370 0

10 9 8 7 6 5 4 3

A CIP catalogue record for this title is available from the British Library

Typeset by Dorchester Typesetting Group Ltd
Printed and bound in Great Britain by Cox & Wyman Ltd, Reading, Berkshire

Contents

For Gina,

from start to finish.

The Gnomecoming Party

Last week of term, see? So the orders are raining down. 'I want all of these lockers cleared by Friday.' 'If there's as much lost property in this cupboard next week as there is now, you lot are going to have some very irritated parents.'

Go home and it's worse. 'You realise you're going to have to *vacuum* this carpet when you've finished unloading that school junk on to it, don't you?' 'I hope you don't think you're just going to add one more archaeological layer to the rubbish already festering in that cupboard. Just clear out the whole lot and sort it properly.'

No point in arguing. So I set to and got on with it. It was like boot camp. Fresh commands kept hurtling over. 'Anything you've grown out of in this pile, please.' 'Surely at least some of these old toys could go to Oxfam? You never play with them.'

But they're still *mine*. Carefully I raised the lid of my huge box of building bits to make sure Mum hadn't been doing any secret clearing of her own. No, there they all were – shoals of brightly-coloured plastic rectangles with those knobbly bits across the top that stick them to the next piece. I scooped up a couple of handfuls to hear that sweet clattery all-the-bits-tipped-on-the-carpet-at-once sound one more time.

And that's when I found him. I saw his little pointy cap first. But when I dug my hands in deeper and fished him out, there he was, all of him: Geoffrey the Gnome.

Geoffrey the next-door's garden gnome, to be precise. I stole him years ago. Let's not get into this blame thing. I know it's wrong to steal – bleh, blehdibleh bleh, etc. – but all I intended at the start was to borrow him. Just for a morning. Then he'd have been back in the Urquharts' garden without anyone even noticing he'd been gone.

It was pottery class, see? And you don't mess with Miss Hooper. You simply do not mess with women like that. If she says she wants everybody's pottery goblin from last week's lesson back for a morning exhibition in the hall, then back it comes.

Except I'd broken mine. Well, I hadn't exactly broken him. I'd left him in the driveway with a little black home-made pit stop flag in his hand to greet my dad when he drove home from work.

'Well, what did you *expect* to happen?' he asked me as I stood forlornly staring at the crumbly bits. 'You surely didn't think I would *notice* it, did you? You can hardly have expected me to have had time to *brake*?'

'It was waving a flag,' I reminded him.

Dad picked up what was left of that. 'James, this flag

is approximately two centimetres by three. I'm not in the habit of driving with night-vision binoculars moulded to my spectacles. Nor do I customarily scour the driveway for artwork as I come in.'

'All right. Keep your hair on,' I told him. 'After all, it's my pottery goblin lying there in splinters. Not yours.'

And it was me, not him, who was going to have to face Miss Hooper's killer stare in the morning. I only did what anyone of the meanest spirit and intelligence would have done. I sneaked round next door and rescued the Urquharts' precious Geoffrey from his dreary, unfulfilling life under their buddleia.

'Come on, Geoffs,' I told him. 'Time to heave your fat, flabby butt off that mushroom and be a bit of use to society.'

I mucked him up a bit. (Miss Hooper knows that I'm no good at pottery.) I shoved a few lumps of wet clay on to the ends of his fingers to make him look lumpy and second-rate. I put a paper cap on to hide the rather stylish way his hat was crumpled. And then I leaned a label with my name against him, shoved him practically out of sight at the back, and kept my fingers crossed till it was clear we'd got away with it and The Mad Potter was finally satisfied enough to let everyone take their poor derided goblin home again for a bit of peace and quiet.

Obviously, I meant to take him back next door at once. It's so long ago now, I can hardly remember what made it so awkward. That workman installing the Urquharts' new movement-sensitive security light can't have helped matters. Or that grousing over the fence. 'Now even Geoffrey's vanished! Believe me, these vandals won't get away with it next time!' I doubt if all that encouraged me to rush into being caught red-handed. I can only presume I shoved Geoffrey safely away in my big box of building bits till I felt brave enough to have a go.

Shame I forgot where I put him so quickly.

Be fair. I never left the Urquharts worrying. When the subject of Geoffrey going AWOL came up again at their boring Christmas drinks party – ('Yes, James. You *do* have to go. It's important to learn to be civil to neighbours.') – I made a real effort, writing a postcard and making Mrs Harrison at school promise faithfully she'd post it with all hers from Mallorca:

REALLY NEEDED A GOOD HOLIDAY AFTER ALL THOSE YEARS IN THE GARDEN. HAVING A WONDERFUL TIME.

LOVE TO ALL AT NO. 27.

GEOFFREY

'Just so my uncle doesn't upset the only neighbours he forgot. This way, they'll simply think their card took longer than all the others to be delivered.'

She was a soft touch – didn't even charge me for the stamp. And since then, Geoffrey's sent the Urquharts postcards from every corner of the globe. He's quite the world traveller. Sometimes I get the local colour up the spout. They were a bit baffled when the card nattered on about sunbathing when he was in Reykjavik. And surfing in Idaho. And luxury hotels in Chad. But that was my fault, handing the cards to perfect strangers who'd missed the Gatwick Express and had to change at East Croydon. Daft of me, really. I should have stuck to what I usually did, bribing my mates at school to sneak them in with their parents' cards. After all, nothing that Geoffrey ever wrote was more of a lie than the sort of stuff they send to friends and family to cheer themselves up about wasting their money: 'Having a simply lovely time here in Vieux Crudville. Locals so friendly. Children loving every minute.'

Well, now I'd found him. Time to give him back. He still looked natty. The lumps of clay I'd shoved all over him to fool Miss Hooper had fallen off. I reckoned he looked quite as good as before, and certainly a whole lot better than if he'd spent the intervening years with little gifts dropping on him from birds on high, and chips taken out of him each time Mr Urquhart came round the buddleia too fast on the mower.

I didn't want to give them heart attacks. So I wrote one last postcard. Before, I'd always dashed these off without much thought, like doing poems for homework. This time I sucked my pencil long and hard. And that's when the big idea flashed up. If I'd been gone for three long years, what would I want?

That's right. A party.

TO ALL MY FRIENDS AT NO. 27. PUT OUT THE
BUNTING! MY TRAVELS ARE OVER. A WISER AND
MORE THOUGHTFUL CREATURE RETURNS TO HIS
SPOTTED MUSHROOM – AND YOU.
YOUR LOVING,
GEOFFREY

Good, eh? I got a man at Purley to promise to post it from Rotherhithe. Then I put up a poster in school:

GOBLIN REUNION!!! CLASS OF 1997!

Mr Hollingdale screeched to a halt in the corridor. 'So what's all this about?'

'Party,' I told him. 'Party for pottery goblins.'

He gave me one of his brain-frying stares. 'Am I to understand that, just as I begin to make headway clearing a term's detritus, you are about to encourage your year group to bring some of the least attractive *objets d'art* ever seen in my classroom back into school?'

'Party, see?' I persisted. 'Party for goblins.'

He laid his hand on my forehead. 'Feeling all right, are you, James?' he asked in that tone that implies, if you are, you soon won't be.

'No, really,' I insisted. 'We all spent hours on those goblins, and all that ever happened was that they sat for a morning on the display table in assembly, with people scoffing at them.'

He looked a little guilty. (He'd scoffed more than most.)

'So,' I said. 'I'm arranging a reunion.'

He went off then, with that strained look of his that seems to say, 'Do nothing rash. Think of your pension.' Everyone else was dead keen. Ted got his goblin back from his granny. Todwell sneaked his away from pride of place on his stepmother's mantelpiece. (My golly, that woman must try hard.) Justin found his in a welly. Lots of the rest surprisingly had theirs still knocking about, holding down attic hatches; propping open cupboard doors – that sort of thing. I was astonished to see how many of the things were staring at me from my locker by Thursday.

Miss Hooper sallies up, poison ducts fully inflated. 'Return of the Uglies, is it?' she asked, making it clear she's referring as much to us as anything stuffed in my locker. She picked up Todwell's. 'What mark did I give this?'

'B,' Tods said, filled with modest pride.

'Mistake, that,' she said, poling off again. 'Should

have been a double detention.' And since she'd done her bit to sour the festive mood, that's when I broke the sad news:

'You're none of you invited, I'm afraid. This party's "Goblins Only".'

Nobody cared a jot. I was quite hurt. No time to brood, though, since it took an hour or more to drag those ugly little pottery beasts all the way up Acacia Avenue. 'Oh, not more stuff!' Mum wailed as I staggered past, weighed down with black bags, a satanic Santa.

But it was worth it. Oh, yes. It was worth it. Worth missing Thursday night's repeat of Morecambe and Wise. (When else would both the Urquharts tell themselves it was only the cat setting all the lights flashing?) Worth staying up till midnight to make the bunting, and creeping out again just before dawn to drape it all over the buddleia. Worth getting my socks scorched off later for pinching Mum's precious collection of economy-class sherry miniatures, and strewing them from the box hedge to the magnolia. Worth sneaking back and forth for half an hour with lumpy, misbegotten party animals that only a desperate stepmother would look at twice.

But, most of all, worth standing there at the window at eight o'clock, knotting my school tie for the last time that term, and seeing everything.

'Lilian! Lilian!' Mr Urquhart was rushing up and down like a madman. 'Our Geoffrey's back! It's Geoffrey! Just like the postcard said! Geoffrey!'

Mrs Urquhart appeared in her nightie. 'Really?'

'Yes, really! Look!'

And so they did. Looked at the tiny little pottery revellers flat out on their lawn. Looked at the dew-soaked banners flapping from laurel to laurel: *WELCOME HOME, GEOFFREY!* Looked at the rather tacky home-made bunting and miniature bottles strewn all around from what had obviously been the world's best homecoming party.

And, most of all, looked at Geoffrey, spruce as before, back on his spotted mushroom.

There was, I thought, a sort of reverent hush about the moments after that. Mum floated up behind me. Together we stared down at Mr and Mrs Urquhart, taking it in turns to clutch Geoffrey to their bosoms and stare in wonder at the squalor round them.

'Could this be anything to do with you?' she asked at last.

I shook my head. 'Mystery!' I assured her, carrying on knotting my tie and pulling on my socks. 'But at least it'll give them something different to talk about over the fence and at their ghastly, boring Christmas party.'

She gave me a beady look I took to mean, 'Don't think you've heard the last of this.'

But it was obviously not the time. After all, she had to get to work, and I had school. And there'll be time enough to face the music. Eight in the morning is not the perfect hour of day for long confessions, explanations and apologies.

And, today of all days, it's important to be first in the queue for assembly.

It's end of term, see? And about time too.

Very Different

'Mum,' I said. 'Tell me the story of how you were born.'

'I've told you before.'

'So tell me again.'

She wasn't busy. She was just sitting on the sofa behind me, disapproving while I did my eyes with my new aubergine stuff. I could see her in the mirror.

'Get on with it, then,' I ordered. 'I'm off out soon.'

'Then you haven't time to hear it all over again.'

'Yes, I have.'

To prove it, I dropped down on the rug in a perfect lotus, my back completely straight. She didn't send me to all those ballet lessons for nothing. Mum made a face. She hates it when I do that. She says it makes her feel a hundred years old.

'Go on, then,' I told her, and reached for the nail polish bottles. I'd bought them that morning. They were lovely. Smoked glass, and shaped like roly-poly little moonmen. I stood them by my bare feet, tiny fat sentries, while I did my toes. They didn't have any labels. To tell what colour the polish was, you had to look into their big round eyes. The one by my left foot had apple green eyes, and the one by my right foot had silver.

'You take care not to drip that stuff over the carpet,' Mum nagged me.

'Get on with the *story*,' I told her. 'How you were born.'

'You told me you were leaving at seven to see a film about weevils taking over the Falklands.'

'Not weevils,' I said. 'Giant cockroaches. And not the

Falklands, either. The Channel Islands. Out of season.'

'*You're* out of season,' Mum scolded. She meant my dress. And there's not that much to it, I have to admit. Dad won't even let me wear it when I'm at his house. He says I might just as well go about stark naked. Mum's not that keen on it, either. She sighs and says there's no point *saying* anything. Then she goes on to say it all the same. But I still wear the dress.

'If you don't get on with the story right now,' I warned, 'I'll wear it without the shoulder straps.'

Mum hates it when I wear it without the shoulder straps. She thinks it will fall off if I sneeze. She got on with the story pretty sharpish.

'Your granny and grandpa had known one another for a number of years. They started courting seriously on bonfire night one year. And it was only a matter of time, a year at most, before they became very close.'

I kept my head down over my shining toes and shook my hair around my face, but she still caught me grinning.

'Listen,' she said. 'This is your grandparents we're talking about. My father and mother. Things were different then. Very different.'

'You're telling me,' I chortled. I *love* this story.

Mum simply decided to ignore me.

'Both of them thought, right from the very start, that they would get married some day. And they were very much in love, so, as I said, they became close.'

'*Very* close, you said.'

'Very close, then.'

I stopped painting my toes. We were getting to one of the best bits.

'Nevertheless,' said Mum, 'they were always most careful to take full precautions.'

I can't help it if I start laughing, can I? It's so *funny*. 'I *love* the way you say that,' I told her. '"Take full precautions".' I rolled the words around my mouth. 'Like rubber pads and plastic gloves and woolly vests and quarantine.' Suddenly I noticed the clock hands, and broke off.

'Go *on*,' I ordered her sternly. 'We haven't got much longer.'

Mum took up the tale with as much dignity as she could muster, pretending she'd never been interrupted.

'So when it became clear that something had gone wrong, they were really shaken and upset. Your grandpa, George, especially. You see, he hadn't really planned on marrying for years, let alone having a baby. George had great dreams, then, for getting just a little bit more experience at Waverley's, then going out to the Persian Gulf, or somewhere, and making his name in a small but expanding engineering firm he'd been told about. And Granny had plans, too, to use a little money her Great Aunt Doe had left her, and open a tiny quilt shop on Ware Street. It was going to be called The Peaceable Kingdom. She'd even designed her own shop sign. It was lovely.'

Her voice trailed off. I know she was remembering the day her mother found the old design inside the pages of a book.

'Poor Granny,' I said. 'Poor Grandpa.'

I meant it. I honestly wasn't just having her on. I don't know why she had to give me that suspicious look before she carried on.

'So they asked a friend for advice, and he gave them the name of this man – a doctor –'

'The friend! Don't miss out the friend! I *love* the seedy friend bit!' But I had to check the clock, and it was too late, I could tell. 'No,' I said. 'It's too near seven. You'll have to skip the seedy friend. We don't have time for him today.'

Mum shook her head in wonder. I think she sometimes thinks she's raised a monster.

'So the next day George and Ellie went off to see this doctor. George was apparently in a dreadful mood. He wouldn't even hold Ellie's hand. He barely spoke. The doctor's name was Fowler, Dr Charles Fowler. He lived in a lovely old house, one of the ones they uprooted to make way for that nasty new Tesco's. His waiting-room was up a lot of steps. It was a white waiting-room, and unheated. Your granny said she felt quite cold.'

'Shiver, shiver!' (I, of course, know what's coming next.)

'And although they were the only people in there, it was at least half an hour before the receptionist showed them into the surgery. Dr Fowler apologised for keeping them waiting, and asked them both to sit down. He even drew out a chair for Ellie. Then he walked round and sat at the other side of his desk, about as close as you are to me right now.'

I sat quite, quite still. This is the best bit.

'They both liked him enormously, right from the start. He was very sympathetic, very professional. Fatherly, I suppose. He asked after Ellie's dates, and then he wanted to know if there were any other symptoms.

He checked on everything, every small detail. He was so careful. He said they might not believe it, but some doctors made a tidy living on the side "helping out" young women who thought, quite mistakenly, that they were pregnant.

'And he was perfectly frank and open about money. He said that since the two of them had been sensible enough to seek help without delay, he would only have to charge them seventy pounds, which was the very minimum, payable in advance, with absolutely no extras at all. He said that he could almost guarantee that there would be no complications. Ellie was obviously a healthy young woman. And although she would have to go overnight into a special nursing home, that was really just to be extra careful, since it was actually a very simple operation.

'Ellie could see that George was most impressed with him. I think they'd both thought that, since the whole business was so forbidden and illegal, they'd have to deal with a very different type. Very different. So George nodded, and Ellie nodded, and Dr Fowler nodded. And then, when everyone had nodded round at everyone else, Dr Fowler said he'd see what he could do to fix the whole business up quickly, so a nice couple like them didn't have to sit around worrying themselves sick about when it would be.'

You watch Mum's face when she tells this bit.

'So then Dr Fowler picked up the telephone on his desk and started to dial the number of the nursing home, while George and Ellie smiled bravely at one another and felt better about things than they had in a fortnight. But the nursing home took its time answering. The room was quiet, not even a clock ticking, and they could hear the ringing tone quite clearly, even though Dr Fowler was holding the receiver to his ear.'

She stopped. She always stops at this bit. It's so weird.

'Go on,' I said. 'And then –'

'And then someone answered – at least, that's what they thought, of course, because Dr Fowler began to speak. "Hello, matron. How are you? . . . Well, that's good . . . Fine. Now listen, matron. I have a young couple with me here now who have just got themselves into a bit of a fix," – and here he winked across your grandmother's head at George.'

'Pig!' I whispered. I *hate* old Dr Fowler at this bit. I just *hate* him. 'Sexist pig!'

'And just at that moment, as he was winking at your grandfather, the two of them heard the ringing tone again, faint but perfectly clear, coming out of the earpiece of the receiver.'

'Brrrrrrrr-brrrrrrrrrrrr.' (I always do this bit for her.) 'Brrrrrrrr-brrrrrrrrrrrr.' Creepy!

'And your granny looked across at George, and George looked back at her. He had heard it too, you see. And she says she remembers putting her hands across her stomach –'

'Across *you*.'

'Well, yes. As it later turned out. Across me. And she remembers that she thought: "Oh, well".'

'Just that? "Oh, well"?' (I find this bit so hard to believe. But that's what Mum always says Granny always told her.)

'Yes. Just, "Oh, well". She says she couldn't think any further, not just then, for all the time that frightful man was chatting away into the telephone: "You mean you actually have a spare bed there right now, matron? . . . A sudden cancellation? . . . Well, that would be perfect. Shall we settle for four o'clock, then? . . . Fine . . . Fine." And all through, in the pauses, they could still hear that tiny ringing going on and on and on.'

'Oooooh!' I can hardly bear to think about it. It sends the shivers all over me. 'Ooooooh!'

'Then George stood up and held out his hand to Ellie, and both of them walked straight out of the surgery, just like that, without a word. They left Dr Fowler sitting behind his desk with the receiver in his hand still giving off those tell-tale little sounds. And they went through the empty waiting-room, and down the stairs to the street, where George turned to Ellie and said: "I suppose that's curtains for the Persian Gulf, then," and Ellie nodded, feeling a bit sorry about the quilt shop, too. So they walked straight into the first restaurant they saw and bought a simply wonderful supper with some of the money George had borrowed that morning to pay the doctor.'

'And they never thought of asking around again?'

'It was difficult in those days. It was completely and totally against the law. If you got caught, you went to prison.'

'And so they just got married.'

'Yes.'

'And you were born seven months later.'

'That's right.'

'Amazing. It's absolutely *amazing*,' I said. (I always do.)

'I don't see why, particularly,' says Mum. (She always does.) 'That's how things *were*, back then.'

And I try to explain.

'All those *dreams*,' I say. 'All those *plans*. Grandpa's Persian Gulf, and Granny's Peaceable Kingdom. All up in smoke, just like that. Ending up married with a baby, just because of a ringing tone.' I give myself a little shake. 'It could *never* happen nowadays.'

'I told you,' Mum says. 'Things were different then. Very different.'

The clock struck seven. I had to go. I hate missing the start of a film. I rose and put the two roly-poly nail polish bottles side by side on the mantelpiece. They stood together, green and silver-eyed.

'They're like people from Mars,' I said. 'That's what they're like.'

'Who? Granny and Grandpa? Or your little glass bottles?'

I didn't answer that. (Not sure I knew!)

'Bye-ee,' I said, leaning down to plant a great smacker on Mum's cheek. 'Be good. And thanks for the story.'

Mum sighed.

'When *I* was young,' she said, 'daughters asked mums to tell them *proper* stories.'

I couldn't help grinning.

'Oh, well,' I told her. 'Things were different then, weren't they? Very different.'

Fabric Crafts

Alastair MacIntyre gripped his son Blair by the throat and shook him till his eyes bulged.

'Look here, laddie,' he hissed. 'I'm warning ye. One more time, say that one more time and whatever it is ye think ye're so good at, *whatever*, I'll have ye prove it!'

'You let go of Blair at once,' said Helen MacIntyre. 'His breakfast's getting cold on the table.'

Giving his son one last fierce shake, Alastair MacIntyre let go. Blair staggered backwards and caught his head against the spice shelf. Two or three little jars toppled over and the last of the turmeric puffed off the shelf and settled gently on his dark hair.

Alastair MacIntyre heard the crack of his son's head against the wood and looked up in anguish.

'Did ye hear that? Did ye hear that, Helen? He banged his head on yon shelf. He couldnae have done that a week back. The laddie's still growing! It'll be new trousers in another month. Och, I cannae bear it, Helen! I cannae bear to watch him sprouting out of a month's wages in clothes before my eyes. I'd raither watch breakfast telly!'

And picking up his plate, he left the room.

Blair fitted his long legs awkwardly under the table and rubbed his head.

'What was all that about?' he asked his mother. 'Why did he go beserk? What happened?'

'You said it again.'

'I didnae!'

'You did.'

'How? When?'

'You came downstairs, walked through the door, came up behind me at the stove, looked over my shoulder at the bacon in the pan, and you said it.'

'I didnae.'

'You did, lamb. You said: "I bet I could fit more slices of bacon into the pan than that." That's what you said. That's when he threw himself across the kitchen to throttle you.'

'I didnae hear myself.'

Helen MacIntyre put her hands on her son's shoulders and raised herself on to her tiptoes. She tried to blow the turmeric off his hair, but she wasn't tall enough.

'No. You don't hear yourself. And you don't think before you speak either. I reckon all your fine brains are draining away into your legs.'

'Blair doesnae have any brains.' Blair's younger sister, Annie, looked up from her crunchy granola. 'If he had any brains, he wouldnae say the things he does.'

'I dinnae say them,' Blair argued. 'They just come

out. I dinnae even hear them when they're said!'

'There you are,' Annie crowed. 'That's what Mum said. All legs, no brain.'

She pushed her plate away across the table and dumped her school bag in its place. 'Tuesday. Have I got everything I need? Swimsuit, gym shorts, metalwork goggles, flute and embroidery.'

'Wheesht!' Blair warned. 'Keep your voice down.' But it was too late. The cheery litany had brought Alastair MacIntyre back into the doorway like the dark avenging angel of some ancient, long-forgotten educational system.

'Are ye quite sure ye've no' forgotten anything?' he asked his daughter with bitter sarcasm. 'Skis? Sunglasses? Archery set? Saddle and bridle, perhaps?'

'Och, no!' said Annie. 'I won't be needing any of them till it's our class's turn to go to Loch Tay.'

Alastair MacIntyre turned to his son.

'What about you, laddie? Are you all packed and

ready for a long day in school? Climbing boots? Bee-keeping gear? Snorkel and oxygen tank?'

'Tuesday,' mused Blair. 'Only Fabric Crafts.'

'Fabric Crafts?'

'You know,' his wife explained to him. 'Sewing. That useful little skill you never learned.'

'Sewing? A laddie of mine sitting at his desk, sewing?'

'No, Dad. We dinnae sit at our desks. We have to share the silks and cottons. We sit round in a circle, and chat.'

'Sit in a circle and sew and chat?'

Blair backed away.

'Mam, he's turning rare red. I hope he's no' going to try again to strangle me!'

Alastair MacIntyre put his head in his hands.

'I cannae believe it,' he said in broken tones. 'My ain laddie, the son and grandson of miners, sits in a sewing circle and chats.'

'I dinnae just chat. I'm very good. I've started on

embroidery now I've finished hemming my apron!'

Alastair MacIntyre groaned.

'His apron!'

'Dinnae take on so,' Helen MacIntyre comforted her husband. 'Everyone's son does it. The times are changing.' She tipped a pile of greasy dishes into the sink and added: 'Thank God.'

'Not *my* son!' Alastair MacIntyre cried. 'Not *my* son! Not embroidery! No! I cannae bear it! I'm a reasonable man. I think I move with the times as fast as the next man. I didnae make a fuss when my ain lassie took up the metalwork. I didnae like it, but I bore with it. But there are limits. A man must have his sticking place, and this is mine. I willnae have my one and only son doing embroidery.'

'Why not?' demanded Blair. 'I'm very good at it. I bet I can embroider much, much better than wee Annie here.'

A terrible silence fell. Then Annie said: 'Ye said it again!'

Blair's eyes widened in horror. 'I didnae!'

'You did. We all heard ye. You said: "I bet I can embroider much, much better than wee Annie here!" '

'I didnae!'

'Ye did.'

'Mam?'

Mrs MacIntyre reached up and laid a comforting hand on his shoulder.

'Ye did, lamb. I'm sorry. I heard it, too.'

Suddenly Alastair MacIntyre looked as if an unpleasant thought had just struck him. He quickly recovered himself and began to whistle casually. He reached over to the draining-board and picked up his lunch box. He slid his jacket off the peg behind the door, gave his wife a surreptitious little kiss on the cheek and started sidling towards the back door.

'Dad!'

Alastair MacIntyre pretended not to have heard.

'Hey, *Dad*!'

Even a deaf man would have felt the reverberations. Alastair MacIntyre admitted defeat. He turned back to his daughter.

'Yes, hen?'

'What about what you told him?'

'Who?'

'Blair.'

'What about, hen?'

'About what would happen if he said it again.'

Alastair MacIntyre looked like a hunted animal. He loosened his tie and cleared his throat, and still his voice came out all ragged.

'What did I say?'

'You said: "Say that one more time and whatever it is ye think ye're so good at, *whatever*, I'll have ye prove it." That's what you said.'

'Och, weel. This doesnae count. The laddie cannae prove he sews better than you.'

'Why not?'

'He just cannae.'

'He can, too. I'm entering my embroidery for the end of term competition. He can enter his.'

'No, lassie!'

'Yes, Dad. You said so.'

'I was only joking.'

'Dad! You were not!'

Alastair MacIntyre ran his finger round his collar to loosen it, and looked towards his wife for rescue.

'Helen?'

Annie folded her arms over her school bag and looked towards her mother for justice.

'Mam?'

Mrs MacIntyre turned away and slid her arms, as she'd done every morning for the last nineteen years, into the greasy washing-up water.

'I think,' she said, 'it would be very good for him.'

Alastair MacIntyre stared in sheer disbelief at his wife's back. Then he slammed out. The heavy shudder of the door against the wooden frame dislodged loose plaster from the ceiling. Most of it fell on Blair, mingling quite nicely with the turmeric.

'Good for me, nothing,' said Blair. 'I'd enjoy it.'

'I didnae mean good for you,' admitted Mrs MacIntyre. 'I meant it would be good for your father.'

It was with the heaviest of hearts that Alastair MacIntyre returned from the pithead that evening to find his son perched on the doorstep, a small round embroidery frame in one hand, a needle in the other, mastering stem stitch.

'Have ye no' got anything better to do?' he asked his son irritably.

Blair turned his work over and bit off a loose end with practised ease.

'Ye know I've only got a week, Dad. I'm going to have to work night and day as it is.'

Alastair MacIntyre took refuge in the kitchen. To try to

cheer himself, he said to Helen: 'Wait till his friends drap in to find him ta'en up wi' yon rubbish. They'll take a rise out o' the laddie that will bring him back into his senses.'

'Jimmy and Iain were here already. He sent them along to The Work Box on Pitlochrie Street to buy another skein of Flaming Orange so he could finish off his border of French knots.'

The tea mug shook in Alastair MacIntyre's hand. 'Och, no,' he whispered.

Abandoning his tea, he strode back into the hall, only to find his son and his friends blocking the doorway as they held one skein of coloured embroidery floss after another up to the daylight.

'Ye cannae say that doesnae match. That's perfect, that is.'

'Ye maun be half blind! It's got a heap more red in it than the other.'

'It has not. It's as yellowy as the one he's run out of.'

'It is not.'

'What about that green, then? That's perfect, right?'

'Aye, that's unco' guid, that match.'

'Aye.'

Clutching his head, Alastair MacIntyre retreated.

The next day, Saturday, he felt better. Ensconsed in his armchair in front of the rugby international on the television, his son at his side, he felt a happy man again – till he looked round.

Blair sat with his head down, stitching away with a rather fetching combination of Nectarine and Baby Blue.

'Will ye no' watch the match?' Alastair MacIntyre snapped at his son.

'I am watching,' said Blair. 'You should try watching telly and doing satin stitch. It's no' the easiest thing.'

Alastair MacIntyre tried to put it all out of his mind. France versus Scotland was not a match to spoil with parental disquiet. And when, in the last few moments, the beefy fullback from Dunfermline converted the try that saved Scotland's bacon, he bounced in triumph on the springs of his chair and shouted in his joy: 'Son, did ye see that? Did ye see that?'

'Sorry,' said Blair. 'This coral stitch is the very de'il. Ye cannae simply stop and look up halfway through.'

All through the night, Alastair MacIntyre brooded. He brooded through his Sunday breakfast and brooded through his Sunday lunch. He brooded all through an afternoon's gardening and through most of supper. Then, over a second helping of prunes, he finally hatched out a plan.

The next evening, when he drove home from the pithead, instead of putting the car away in the garage he parked it in front of the house – a K-registration Temptress – and went in search of his wayward son. He found him on the upstairs landing, fretting to Annie about whether his cross stitches were correctly aligned.

'Lay off that, laddie,' Alastair MacIntyre wheedled. 'Come out and help me tune up the car engine.'

Blair appeared not to have heard. He held his work up for his father's inspection.

'What do you reckon?' he said. 'Be honest. Dinnae spare my feelings. Do ye think those stitches in the China Blue are entirely regular? Now look very closely. I want ye to be picky.'

Alastair MacIntyre shuddered. Was this his son? He felt as if an incubus had taken hold of his first-born.

'Blair,' he pleaded. 'Come out to the car. I need your help.'

'Take wee Annie,' Blair told him. 'She'll help ye. She got top marks in the car maintenance module. I cannae come.'

'Please, laddie.'

Alastair MacIntyre was almost in tears.

Blair rose. Extended to his full height, he towered over his father.

'Dad,' he said. 'Take wee Annie. I cannae come. I

cannae risk getting oil ingrained in my fingers. It'll ruin my work.'

Barely stifling his sob of humiliation and outrage, Alastair MacIntyre took the stairs three at a time on his way down and out to the nearest dark pub.

He came home to find wee Annie leaning over his engine, wiping her filthy hands on an oily rag.

'Ye've no' been looking after it at all well,' she scolded him. 'Your sparking plugs were a disgrace. And how long is it since you changed the oil, I'd like to know.'

Mortified, feeling a man among Martians, Alastair MacIntyre slunk through his own front door and up to his bed.

On the morning of the school prize-giving, Alastair MacIntyre woke feeling sick. He got no sympathy from his wife, who lay his suit out on the double bed.

Alastair MacIntyre put his head in his hands.

'I cannae bear it!' he said. 'I cannae bear it. My ain son, winning first prize for Fabric Crafts, for his sewing! I tell you, Helen. I cannae bear it!'

He was still muttering 'I cannae bear it' over and over to himself as the assistant head teacher ushered the two of them to their seats in the crowded school hall. The assistant head teacher patted him on the back in an encouraging fashion and told him: 'You maun be a very proud man today, Mr MacIntyre.'

Alastair MacIntyre sank on to his seat, close to tears.

He kept his eyes closed for most of the ceremony, opening them only when Annie was presented with the Junior Metalwork Prize, a new rasp. Here, to prove he was as much a man of the times as the next fellow, he clapped loudly and enthusiastically, then shut his eyes again directly, for fear of seeing his only son presented with a new pack of needles.

When the moment of truth came, he cracked and

peeped. Surreptitiously he peered around at the other parents. Nobody was chortling. Nobody was whispering contemptuously to a neighbour. Nobody was so much as snickering quietly up a sleeve. So when everyone else clapped, he clapped too, so as not to seem churlish.

Somebody leaned forward from the row behind and tapped on his shoulder.

'I wadna say but what ye maun be a proud faither today, Alastair MacIntyre.'

And raw as he was, he could discern no trace of sarcasm in the remark.

As they filed out of the hall, Annie and Blair rejoined them. Alastair MacIntyre congratulated his daughter. He tried to follow up this success by congratulating his son, but the words stuck in his throat. He was rescued by the arrival, in shorts and shirts, of most of the school football team.

'Blair! Are ye no' ready yet? We're waitin' on ye!'

The goalie, a huge burly lad whose father worked at

the coal face at Alastair MacIntyre's pit, suddenly reached forward and snatched at Blair's embroidery. Blair's father shuddered. But all the goalie did was start to fold it up neatly.

'A fair piece o' work, that,' he said. 'I saw it on display in yon hall. I dinnae ken how you managed all them fiddly bits.'

'Och, it was nothing,' said Blair. 'I bet if you tried, you could do one just as guid.'

Alastair MacIntyre stared at his son, then his wife, then his daughter, then his son again.

'Och, no,' demurred the goalie. 'I couldnae manage that. I've no' got your colour sense.'

He handed the embroidery to Alastair MacIntyre.

'Will ye keep hold o' that for him?' he said. 'He's got to come and play football now. We cannae wait any longer.' He turned to Annie. 'And you'll have to come too, wee Annie. Neil's awa' sick. You'll have to be the referee.'

Before she ran off, Annie dropped her new rasp into one of her father's pockets. Blair dropped a little packet into the other.

Alastair MacIntyre jumped as if scalded.

'What's in there?' he demanded, afraid to reach in and touch it in case it was a darning mushroom, or a new thimble.

'Iron-on letters,' Blair said. 'I asked for them. They're just the job for football shirts. We learned to iron in Home Economics. I'm going to fit up the whole football team.'

'What with?'

'KIRKCALDIE KILLERS,' Blair told him proudly. 'In Flaming Orange and Baby Blue.'

Getting the
Messages

How did I tell them? How does anybody tell them? It was a mixture of chance, and being up to here with the sheer awfulness of them not having a clue. (I'm not kidding. I don't think it had even crossed their minds.) I was a wreck from walking through our back door every day after school, practically expecting to see their pale shocked faces raised to mine. Sooner or later one of life's meddlers was going to take a swing at them with the old wet sock of truth, and come out with a helpful little 'I really thought it was time someone told you.' After all, most of my friends knew. And once Mr Heffer had soft-soled his way up behind me in the newsagent's while I was flicking through something pretty dubious, I was pretty sure all the staff were in on it (and half the dinner ladies, if that strange rumour about Mr Heffer has any truth to it). I even reckoned Mr Faroy the grocer had guessed, and I'm not sure he even knows quite what we're talking about.

So that just left them, really. Mum and Dad.

Like everyone else, though, I kept putting it off, not just from cowardice, but from not being sure quite what was driving me towards the dread day of reckoning. I wouldn't be surprised if axe-murderers have the same problem. They escape undetected from the scene of the crime, and then each knock, each phone ring, causes such a rush of stomach-clenching fear that in the end they realise one day soon they're going to walk into some police station – any police station – and give themselves up, just to be able to stretch out on their hard prison bed, and breathe in peace.

Not the best reason for confessing, perhaps. But good

enough. And better than some of the others, like wanting to stop your parents making their tired old jokes about gay presenters on the telly, or simply upset them out of childish spite.

And I certainly didn't want to upset mine. I'm very fond of them, I really am. (Go on. Have a good laugh. I'll wait till you're ready.) I think they're both softies, if you want to know. And I'm the light of Mum's life. Even at my age, they're still checking on me all the time. 'All right, are you, son?' 'Good day at school, sweetheart?' That sort of thing. Not that I'm actually looking for chances to whinge about that animal Parker hurling my sandwiches into the Art room clay bin, or Lucy Prescott stalking me down corridors. But, if I wanted to, I could.

But I couldn't tell them this. Each time I geared myself up, I'd get some horror-show vision in my head of how they might take it. You only need half an ear hanging off one side of your head to know how some parents react. Flora knows someone whose mum wailed on for weeks about it all being *her* fault, then threw herself under a bus. That's something nice for Flora's friend to think about all her life. George has a neighbour whose son was banished. Banished! It sounds medieval, but it happened only last year. And I just read a novel where the father got drunk and cut the little circle of his son's face out of every single family photograph, and dropped the whole lot down the pan. The poor boy pads along to the bathroom in the middle of the night, and finds a little whirlpool of his own unflushed faces staring up at him. Maybe the author made that story up. I certainly hope so.

And then there's Mick. We met on holiday last summer and mooched around together quite a bit. When his dad won the accumulator at the races, and Mick clapped him on the back, he made a flinchy little face and moved away. I bet a heap Mick wishes he'd kept his trap shut.

So you can see why I kept putting it off. But we

couldn't go on for ever. I was sick of not being able to do the simplest things, like keep a proper diary, or snap at Grandpa when he makes remarks about the couple on the corner, or leave the books I'm reading lying about.

And that's how I told them. With a book. Not quite the way you'd imagine, but it worked. Mum and I were in Readerama a few weeks ago, and she was desperate not to let me out of sight because I was carrying most of the shopping. She didn't trust me not to put it down. Mum's of the view that trailing half a step behind every single shopper in town is a villain just waiting to pounce on their Priceworthy carriers, and make off down some dark alley. 'Have you got all the bags? You're supposed to have *six*,' she says to me every two minutes, and I've known her have breakdowns just from my slipping one half empty carrier inside another without sending her warning letters in triplicate first. She drives me mad. And she has the nerve to claim she's not that keen on me, when we're in town together. But I still get dragged along, as unpaid porter, whenever Dad's not available. It's my brute strength she's after, not my advice on broccoli versus sweetcorn, or red versus green for the new lavatory brush holder or, as on this particular morning, which cookery book to buy for Aunty Sarah's birthday.

'Just take the cheapest,' I said. 'It's not as if she ever gets round to actually cooking anything out of them, after all. She just flicks through them and then does chicken and chips.'

'What if she has it already?'

'Give her the receipt. Then she can bring it back and choose another. That way, *she* gets to be the one whose arms stretch down to the floor.'

Mum took the hint. 'All right,' she said unwillingly. 'You can put down the shopping. But don't move away from it. Stay where you are.'

'So what am I supposed to do?'

'Browse,' said my mother. 'That's what people do in bookshops. Have a little browse.'

I browsed. I browsed a step or so to the left (Health Matters). I browsed a step or so to the right (Feminism). I browsed forward a couple of steps (Family and Society), and back a few steps (Cars and Mechanical). And all the time I swear to God I never let a soul get between me and the shopping bags.

Then I got uppity. I browsed a little further away, past Holiday Guides, and round the back of Stamp Collecting. I ended up opposite Food and Drink and, copping a major glower from Mum, who was still choosing which of the eight million cookery books on display Aunty Sarah wouldn't change first, I doubled back through Computers.

Fetching up back at Health Matters, where I'd begun.

That's when I saw it. *Telling Your Parents: A Teenager's Guide to Coming Out in the Family.* You'd think the fairies might have put it there for me. I didn't do what you'd expect – slip it out and have a quick read while she was busy comparing *Feasts of Malaysia* with *You and Your Wok*, then creep back a few days later to read the rest. No. I simply took it off the shelf and tucked it under my arm. Then I dribbled the shopping bags one by one over to Mum at Gluttons' Corner, and stood there growing a beard down to my feet until she'd chosen.

'Right!' she said finally. 'I think this one's nice. She can't complain about this one.'

She waited for me to point out that Aunty Sarah can complain about anything. But I had bigger fish to fry.

I trailed her to the pay desk.

'Here,' she said, taking out her switch card and putting *Winter Cookery: A Casserole Lover's Collection* down on the counter.

'Here,' I said, laying *Telling Your Parents: A Teenager's Guide to Coming Out in the Family* straight down on top of it.

'What's that?'

'A book.'

'What book?' she said, playing for time as if she couldn't read.

'This book,' I said to her firmly. 'This book here.'

'Take it away, Gregory!' Her voice had shot up in the stratosphere. She was positively squeaking. And the poor girl at the pay desk didn't know where to look. (Would I have done it if it had been a bloke on duty that morning? Don't ask. I'll never know.)

'I mean it, Gregory!' Her hand shot out. The book went sailing off the desk on to the floor. 'I'm not buying that for you!'

I felt so sorry for her. But still I picked it up again and put it down on top of *Winter Cookery.*

'No, Gregory! No!' She swiped it off again.

I picked it up. 'Come on, Mum.'

Snatching it from me, she hurled it on the table to the side. 'No! *No!*'

'Yes, Mum,' I said, picking it up a third time.

'Oh, no! Oh, no! Oh, God, Gregory!' She reached for the book, but this time the salesgirl dived forward at the same time, maybe to pitch in on my side, maybe to save the book from yet another battering. When their hands met, the book slid off again on to the floor, falling open at a section called 'Telling the Grandparents'.

'Oh, God!' she wailed. 'I can't believe this is happening!' And I knew from the way it came out that the first of a thousand battles was over. Mum at least believed me.

I've never felt so dreadful in my life. I wanted to say 'I'm sorry', but I was worried she'd misunderstand, and get me wrong about the way I feel. So I said nothing. I just stood there like a giant lump, watching my own mum crumple, thanks to me.

Staff training at Readerama must be brilliant. Not only can the sales force read upside-down, but they know what to do at sticky moments. Glancing at the name on Mum's card, the girl said gently, 'Mrs Fisher, would you like to come through to the back and sit down for a moment? I could make you some coffee.'

Good thing it was my mum I'd dumped the

newsflash on, and not my dad. He'd have dissolved into a puddle of tears and sat there for a week, weeping into his teacup. Mum's made of sterner stuff. She's kept her chin up through some moments of high embarrassment while raising me, and though this must have been about the worst, she still proved equal to the strain.

'That's very nice of you,' she said, pulling her coat straight and clutching her handbag closer. 'Most kind and thoughtful. But I'll be all right.'

The girl gave me a look, and pointed to one of those little stool things they use for getting to the upper shelves. I fetched it over. 'At least sit down,' she said to Mum. 'Just for a moment.'

'Just while you ring up the books, then,' Mum said, collapsing.

'Books', not 'book'. Did you notice? I did. So did the girl.

'It won't take a moment,' she said. But then she made a point of taking her time, sliding the card through the machine the wrong way once or twice, and rooting underneath the counter for a different sized bag, to give my mum a few moments. She even came out from behind the pay desk with the slip, and brought it over for Mum to sign. Mum's hand was shaking, but the signature looked close enough.

'There,' said the girl, managing to make it sound like 'There, there . . .' and making me vow I'll never in my life buy any book in any shop on the planet but Readerama.

Mum raised her head. 'Well, Gregory. We can't stay here all day. Better get home.'

And tell your dad, she might have added. But I wasn't quite so worried about that. Dad has a flaming temper, but in the end he always buys Mum's line on everything. He wasn't going to like it. Well, who would? Like anyone else, he'd like his son to grow up and marry and have a couple of kids, and not be different in any way. But not because the only thing he cares about is my being 'normal'. More because he's quite sure that being different

– especially this way – is going to make absolutely everything in my life a whole lot more difficult for me. Once he's convinced this is the only way I'm going to be, he'll get a grip. He wants me happy more than he wants me straight. I'm lucky there. Some people want you straight a whole lot more than they want you happy.

The bus ride home was pretty quiet (if you don't count Mum saying, 'Gregory, have you got all the bags?' two dozen times). Once or twice, she touched my hand, as if she were about to say something. But it was not till we were walking into our own street that she came out with it.

'Let's not say anything about all this just for the moment.'

I gave her a suspicious look. What was she thinking? I wasn't old enough to know my mind? That this was something I was trying on, like some new style, or haircut? Did she think I was temporarily unhinged? Under someone's spell? Totally mistaken?

'Just for the moment,' she repeated. 'Just till we're sure.'

No point in climbing out of a box if you're going to climb straight back in again. 'I am sure. I've been sure for years now.'

'Well, waiting a little longer before you tell your father won't hurt, then, will it?'

'Mum,' I said. 'Give me one good reason not to tell him now.'

She looked quite hunted. 'You know how upset he's going to be, and we can't have him saying anything in front of Granny and Grandpa.'

Whoah, there! I stopped in my tracks. 'And why not?'

She stopped as well. 'Gregory, you know perfectly well why not.'

I put down the shopping, all six bags of it. 'Mum, you can't pick and choose who I keep this secret from,' I told her. 'It's too important. That has to be *my* decision.'

'But what if your grandpa finds out?'

'It's not a matter of him "finding out",' I said. 'Somebody has to tell him. Otherwise I'll be back exactly where I was before, having to watch myself all the time.'

'Is that so terrible?'

'Yes, it is!' I snapped. 'And it won't stop there, either. Within a week or so, you and Dad will be trying to kid yourselves it was all just a horrible mistake. No, I'm sorry, Mum. I'm not going back and it isn't fair to ask me.'

'Fair?' she hissed, striding off down the street again. '*Fair*? And what about what's fair on the rest of us? You'll give your grandpa a heart attack!'

I'd got her there. 'Oh, I don't think so,' I said, picking up everything and trailing after her. 'Didn't he go ballistic when you told him that Ginny was pregnant by Wayne Foster? And Gran cried for *weeks*. They were so upset and furious, they didn't even go to the wedding. And now look at them! Gran spends her whole life tangled up in pink knitting wool, and Grandpa won't put the baby down. They're tough. They'll get over it.'

Mum strode on furiously. 'Don't kid yourself they're going to come to terms with this quite so easily!'

'I don't see why not,' I said sullenly. 'They've got used to my terrible hair. And my terrible clothes. And my terrible music. And my terrible friends. And my . . .'

'Gregory! This is a whole lot more important than any of those!'

'Yes!' I yelled back. 'It certainly is! And that's exactly why I can't go on pretending all the time – not at school, and on the team, and with girls, and at home, and at my Saturday jobs, and *everywhere*. There's got to be *somewhere* I can just be *me*.'

Perhaps I'd got through to her. Or perhaps it was because we'd practically reached our own gate. But, suddenly, she seemed to soften a little. 'But surely waiting a little is only sensible. What if you change your mind?'

If this had been school debate, I'd have come back at

her pretty sharpish on that one, saying something like, 'I don't recall you ever saying that you put off marrying Dad in case you found out later that you were lesbian.' But this is my mum, don't forget. If I'd said that, she would have slapped me so hard I'd have gone reeling into Mr Skelley's hedge. So I said nothing.

She peered in my face. 'Oh, Gregory. This is going to take a whole lot of getting used to, and I can tell you one thing. The worst isn't over.'

'It is for me,' I told her quite truthfully.

And what if I did mean the lying, the secrets, the worrying, the pretending? Give me a break! She thought I meant that telling her had been the hardest thing. And that was important to her, you could tell. Shocked and upset as she was, you could still see she took it as a compliment that she mattered most. She took it seriously, the same way she took my blotchy finger painting from nursery, and my cracked pottery jewellery pot from primary school, and my split, wobbly stock cube dispenser from secondary school Woodwork. Her mouth even twitched a little, as if, if she didn't have to go in there and help me through Round Two with Dad, she might even have given me the tiniest of encouraging smiles.

I pushed the gate open. 'Ready?' I said, the same way she always used to say it to me when I was starting at a new school or a new club.

'I suppose so,' she muttered, exactly the same way I must have said it to her so many times before.

On our way up the path, she suddenly stopped and hurled herself into one of my shopping bags. Scattering socks and lightbulbs, she dragged out *Telling Your Parents: A Teenager's Guide*, and hurried off round the side of the house.

I set off in pursuit. 'What are you doing?'

'Stuffing this in the dustbin.'

'What, my *book*?'

But it was already gone, deep under tea leaves and

old carrot peelings.

'It's not *your* book,' she said, slamming the lid down over the horrid mess. 'It's my book. I'm the one who paid for it.' She brushed tea leaves off her hands and added bitterly, 'Though I can't think why. You seem to be managing perfectly well without it.'

'But why shove it in the dustbin?'

'Listen, young man,' she warned me dangerously. 'Don't push your luck. If you're planning on making me *live* the bloody book, I'll be damned if I'll *dust* it.'

I know when a job's done. I just picked up the shopping and followed her in to face more of the music.

Two of These and One of Those

'Is it two of these makes one of those, dear?' Adelaide Hall asked, stretching her bluey-white arthritic fingers across the lunch table to display a handful of the still unfamiliar coins. 'Or am I confusing it with ten of these making two of those?'

Behind her, Federico Algaron Arqueso Perez de Vega sighed inwardly and shifted his clean white serving napkin from one bent arm to the other. It was getting on for three o'clock and he'd heard it all before – many times. He wished the straight-backed old English lady would hurry up and tip him and go, taking her daughter and that unsociable, head-in-a-book granddaughter along with her, before the sultry, long-legged French girl sitting alone at the corner table despaired of him in spite of all his constant and meaningful smiles across the dining-room, finished up her third cup of coffee, and left.

'It's two of these little tinny ones to one of those, dear,' Helen assured her mother. 'And ten of these are worth the same as that big one with the chicken on the back.'

Pheasant, Federico corrected her silently, gritting his teeth and staring balefully out through the open door into the bright, sun-bleached street from which these three were so thoughtlessly keeping him. Not chicken. *Faisán*. Doesn't look a bit like a chicken.

'Doesn't look a bit like a chicken,' said Adelaide, letting the offending coin drop from between her stiffened fingers on to the worn white linen cloth, and peering at it closely. 'Not a bit.'

'Pheasant,' Chloe corrected her grandmother,

without even lifting her eyes from her book. *'Faisán.'*

Adelaide caught Helen's eye briefly across the table, and each of them wished, not for the first time, that Chloe had not come. And that was such a shame, because she had always fitted in so well before. As a small child she had always been good as gold, loving the odd-tasting food, the hot dusty parks and the excitable and friendly, if mysteriously babbling children. Older, she had still enjoyed creeping round in the gloom of the cool and cavernous churches, or miming 'no onions' indefatigably to surly, suspicious street hawkers until they were charmed into sudden understanding and smiles.

This year, unaccountably, everything had been different. As holidaymakers, the three of them no longer meshed happily and tolerantly together, and both Adelaide and Helen felt that Chloe was somehow to blame. Where once they had thought her quiet and amenable, now she seemed sullen and passive; and her once happy gift of suggestion had now gone all wrong. She was forever wanting to stay one hour longer, climb one flight higher, eat one course fewer, not take the bus.

But that wasn't the worst. What upset Adelaide and Helen most was the constant niggling corrective remarks that Chloe had taken to throwing out at them from behind the protective barricade of *Bleak House* – remarks which were later referred to simply as 'one of *those*' in the shorthand of their increasingly frequent little talks about the girl.

But it seemed so unlike Chloe to be downright rude. Perhaps she was unhappy. She was certainly under a great deal of pressure at school, what with all the recent changes in the French and Spanish language modules, and the seemingly endless demands of her English folder. She clearly needed taking out of herself, but neither her mother nor her grandmother had the least idea of how to go about it.

Helen, unknown to Adelaide, had been rather

hoping some nice young man would happen along, to sweep her daughter off her feet (and, more to the point, out of her book), and take her around the city to have a good time. Chloe needed a good time badly, and if the holiday went on like this much longer, so would Helen.

Adelaide, unknown to Helen, had been hoping the very same thing. She had even sacrificed two of her own precious and much-loved siestas to walk her granddaughter around the plaza, past the dress shops, pressing new clothes upon her, rack by rack.

'One of these?' she would wheedle, pointing to the bulging piles of brightly-coloured cotton wrap-around skirts that even Adelaide, for all her difficulties with the currency, could see were horrifically overpriced. And, holding up a fresh and cheerful, if frail-looking, pair of woven sandals, 'How about these?' Anything, rather than see Chloe walk down the Calle Mayor one day longer in those nasty old flip-flops that unfortunately made up in toughness and durability for all they lacked in charm and design, and that dreadful dowdy sundress that she seemed to have been wearing for years.

All in vain. Chloe only relented once. She accepted a plain square brown shoulder bag that Adelaide didn't much care for anyway, and only offered as part of a wide-armed, desperate gesture of invitation to Chloe to choose something – *anything* – from *Cosas de Estío*'s entire summer stock. And then it turned out Chloe only chose that to protect her stained and battered copy of *Bleak House* from further ravages on their next boat trip up the coast.

Chloe now raised this same book just a little higher, so she could finish up her coffee and continue to read without a pause. Thus reminded, Federico glanced anxiously over his shoulder at the sultry French girl, who had by now given up the restless crossing and uncrossing of her lovely legs that had so distracted him all through the serving of the soup course, and taken to glowering into her cup instead. She didn't even see his pleading, amorous look. Her slim brown legs looked even more attractive to him now, splayed as they were, awry, beneath the table, and Federico allowed his mind to wander for a moment, out beyond the bright sun-bleached streets he had been longing for earlier, to the bright sun-bleached sheets on his soft wide bed, and further . . . And when he came to, with just the slightest of flushes on his cheeks, the three of them were at it again.

'They can't be worth that much, surely,' Adelaide was insisting, baffled. 'No more than two of these, or one of those at the very most. Why, only yesterday I gave away a whole handful of them for the tiniest cup of coffee I ever saw in my life.'

'*Demi-tasse*,' Chloe said, without even raising her eyes from *Bleak House*.

'Very likely,' said Adelaide. 'It certainly tasted most bitter.' She looked coldly up at Federico, reproving him for yesterday's waiter's transgressions. 'There was so little in there I could scarcely dampen my lips. And even though I kept my hand out, all the waiter gave me back in change was one of the little tinny ones with the president on.'

The *King*, Federico reprimanded Adelaide sternly and silently behind clenched teeth. *El Rey.*

'The King,' Chloe corrected Adelaide aloud. *'El Rey.'*

Federico caught her eye. He smiled at her in his skilled, almost imperceptible fashion, over *Bleak House*. That made him feel better, but it took Chloe quite aback. It was several seconds after she lowered her eyes again to the text that she managed to pick up Dickens's thread.

Federico had less trouble with Adelaide's.

'Scandalous, isn't it?' she was telling Helen crossly. 'It does so spoil things when you always have to be so very much *on your guard.*'

Federico sighed and shifted his clean white serving napkin back onto the first arm again. He shuffled his feet. Above his head, the minute hand on the dining-room clock crawled towards five past three, and over in the corner the French girl began to make the I-just-can't-wait-any-longer gestures he had been fearing ever since she refused the dessert. He couldn't really blame her. She probably couldn't drink another cup of coffee if it were Adonis himself for whom she were stalling, Federico consoled himself sadly. Even though he had made it himself, and it was very good – for *demi-tasse*, that is.

Inwardly giggling, he eyed the absorbed Chloe regretfully. She would have liked that joke. She was probably the only young woman in the whole dining-room who would have understood it. He gave a brief look round and saw the French girl, more sour than sultry now, pick up her keys and her purse. She didn't look at all in the mood for a joke about coffee.

Federico turned back to stare at Chloe with renewed and quickened interest while Helen and Adelaide steered themselves back once again to the gruelling process of working out the tip. Still watching Chloe, Federico predicted under his breath. He'd heard it all so often, it no longer took all his attention.

Is it two of these to one of those? he predicted.

'Is it two of these to one of those?' asked Adelaide, holding a coin up to the light and inspecting it closely. 'And twenty of these in one of those?'

'Yes, that's it, dear. Now I warn you. You must be *very much on your guard.*'

'Two of these in one of those?' Adelaide repeated, amazed and defeated. 'My, my. I'll never get it straight. How much do I owe you for this boat trip up the coast, then? It's five of these, is it?'

No, it's ten of those, Federico longed to say.

'No, it's ten of those,' said Chloe.

Federico gazed at her in grateful admiration. She really was a rather striking-looking girl, when you came to peer more closely. Those terrible down-at-heel flip-flops and that dreadful bedraggled sundress did a brilliant job of hiding it, but actually she had a very lovely figure, and there was nothing wrong with her face that taking that book from her hands wouldn't cure in an instant.

'Now this coin here in your hand that is worth ten of those,' Helen was warning her mother, 'is very similar indeed to that practically worthless coin by your spoon, and could easily be mistaken. You really must keep a most careful watch.'

Federico glanced down at the table. They were both coins, he could see that. But here all similarity between them seemed to come to an end. Raising his eyebrows, Federico began, impatiently, to fidget.

Helen, suddenly impatient herself, looked up at him. Speaking very slowly and clearly and loudly, as if he were not only foreign but also hard of hearing and half-witted, she asked him, 'How much is this little pile of coins here worth?'

'Oh, *don't* Mum!' cried Chloe, outraged, rising from her seat in her agony and dropping *Bleak House* on to the

table edge, from which it fell, unnoticed, to the floor.
'Please *don't*. Don't ask him about his own *tip*!'

Federico gave her a smile – his most beautiful,
winning smile. And assuming, because of it, that he
could not possibly have understood her mother's
question, Chloe sat down again in her chair and smiled
back at him in huge and happy relief.

She looked quite lovely, he thought.

He gave one last glance over his shoulder at the leggy
French girl. But she was already at the door. The sultry
look had gone worse than sour now. It had positively
curdled.

That settles it, thought Federico.

'That settles it,' Adelaide announced. She wound up
the discussion in the same forcible manner in which she
coped, back home in Manchester, with insolent
tradesmen and the unruly American who rented the
house next door.

'I'm going to give you one of these, young man,' she

told Federico firmly. 'And two of these.' She swept the rest of the coins off the tablecloth into her large canvas bag. 'And not a penny more.'

Peseta, thought Federico. Not penny. *Peseta*. He scooped up the two coins with a grateful yet responsible-sounding murmur of thanks which implied that the combined munificence of the three English ladies would keep himself and his seventeen starving brothers knee-deep in *paella* and *tortillas* for several days.

'*Peseta*,' Chloe corrected her grandmother. 'Not penny. *Peseta*.' She smiled broadly at Federico as she said it.

Federico pulled Adelaide's heavy chair out carefully as she rose. He did the same for Helen. Chloe stood up by herself. Nobody except Chloe noticed when Federico dropped his clean white serving napkin over the battered copy of *Bleak House* which still lay beside her on the floor.

And nobody except Federico noticed when Chloe returned, just a few minutes later, still smiling, to claim it.

Falling Apples

It was Antonia who first realised it was to be another of those days. There the four Cox sisters sat, bolt upright in their accustomed places round the polished table. Their pinafores were tugged straight, their hair tied neatly back. Rosie bobbed in and out as usual, with tilting plates and slopping jugs. But as always on these occasions, Mrs Cox barely noticed the tremulous, maladroit serving maid. She only had eyes for her daughters.

'Antonia! Your elbows!'

Not even the frills of her sleeves had brushed the table top, Antonia was sure. But still she made a show of lifting her arms a little. Safer to appease.

'And, Virginia, smirking is deeply unattractive. Do please try to rid yourself of that mean little smile.'

If there were any expression on her sister's face – and that was doubtful – Antonia knew it would have been nothing more than a fleeting look of sympathy. And only someone keeping their mother's unstintingly sharp watch over the four of them would even have noticed it. So she tried to distract with some light remark to Hester about how the rainbow halo cast by the mirror onto the wall above Virginia's head suited that gentlest of sisters perfectly. But Mrs Cox paid no attention. She was, it seemed, working her way round the table as usual.

'Must you *slump* like that, Lucia? You look like a bag of bones. And, Hester, you have a way of stoking food into your mouth that is almost mechanical. Positively *ugly*.'

Ugly, smirking, slumping, clumsy. On and on it

would go now, all of them knew, till the last tinkle of the little silver bell, and the merciful release. 'Now, Rosie, you may clear.' On afternoons like these, it was as if a witch had come to tea in Mother's place – a witch whom no one and nothing could please, yet who was clearly sly enough to know how to amuse herself.

For no one else round the table could take any pleasure in these grim occasions. And any hint of mutiny – the shadows across Virginia's face, Lucia's little pouts, Antonia's short-lived cries of protest, 'But, Mama!' – and the sharp cords of family authority were nipped even tighter.

'Do you dare to contradict me? Are you determined to provoke?'

When they began, these days of wire-taut nerves and thumping hearts, Antonia couldn't recall. And what she and her sisters were afraid of, she couldn't tell, for no one had ever lifted a hand to any of them, she was sure of that. Especially not their father, who steered clear of any unpleasantness. But as far back as Antonia could remember, their mother had had days like these, when every hail-smashed flower stem found in the garden might just as well have been a pit collapse, each message from the kitchen could have been news of a disaster at war, and each laugh from any daughter was a pure affront.

Her fingertips would fly to her temples. 'Girls! Peace! My head is spinning!' But what excuse is that for passing your own misery on like an overhot plate? And finding solace in it. For Antonia had no doubt that, with the witch presiding over the silver teapot, the baiting of each of the sisters round the table in turn served some relieving purpose, as when, through the long winters in the cold, cold house, Antonia herself pressed her sharp fingernails deep in her palms to draw a little of the pain, just for a moment, from her throbbing chilblains.

And no one could deny Mother knew her trade. Safe in the dark of their shared bed, Antonia and Virginia had agreed it was a mystery how easily she could drain the colour from their faces and fill their eyes with tears. As often as not, she'd start with Hester. Not because she was necessarily the easiest of the sisters to unnerve; more because what bit directly into Hester's heart could be approached through easy conversation. It was, after all, the most natural thing to begin with the weather as a topic. From there, to hunting of course. And, after that, seamlessly to animals in general. A short step to pets. And suddenly, tears would be spurting out of Hester's eyes at that apparently so careless reference to dear, dead Hector, most adored of rabbits.

Or, failing that, it would occur to Mrs Cox to ask her girls which way they'd walked that morning. Today, one passing mention of Home Farm was all it took to do the trick. For how could a girl who had to shut her eyes and be led by her sisters down the path past Jamieson's vegetable plots, even bear open mention of that place where any wheeling gull foolish enough to sail to rest and let itself be trapped, had both wings brutally clipped, and faced a miserable half-life of trawling up and down the furrows, seeking out slugs.

'Such a *shame* . . .' Mother mused, as if the idea had, yet again, occurred to her fresh. 'How those poor creatures must long for sea, and miss the sky!'

And Hester's tears rolled, her own wings equally clipped by the set rule that no one might flee from the table, whatever their distress.

Antonia leaped to her sister's defence. 'Oh, *please*, Mama! Don't let's talk about hateful Mr Jamieson.' But Lucia spoiled her chances of curbing their mother by, in her unthinking and importunate way, going too far. 'Yes, Mother. You absolutely mustn't talk to poor Hester about –'

The target, far from shifting, simply widened.

'Nonsense, Lucia! Hester cannot expect our conversations always to take account of her soft heart. She must learn better self-control. And so must you!'

Ah, this was simplicity itself. For Lucia was 'a brimmer'. To send the fat tears glimmering down her cheeks, all Mother had to do was deepen her frown and remind the poor scrap of all the transgressions born of her precipitous flights around the house and gardens after her precious sister. 'After all, you're no better. Who charged down the pantry passage straight into Maria and broke all those porcelain dishes? Who crashed into my finest rose, and snapped its spine?'

'Do you remember,' Antonia said hastily, 'how it bloomed even better the next year?'

But it was hopeless. Lucia's eyes still filled. And Mrs Cox moved on round the table.

Me, thought Antonia. Now it's my turn.

But she was wrong. Her mother had already turned to Virginia.

'No news from Stanhope, I take it?'

Virginia flushed scarlet. It was, as everyone round the table knew, the deepest of humiliations for her that, so far, no invitation from the Grange had yet arrived. Everyone else seemed to have been invited to the party – even Drusilla Carter. And if a tradesman's daughter was welcome to spend the afternoon lobbing tennis balls over nets and sipping crushed strawberry ices, then their Virginia must have made a very poor impression on her last visit to the Grange, not to be asked back again.

With no control over the colour of her face, Virginia made an effort to keep her voice unruffled.

'Oh, I do hope the weather holds for them. What could be more dismal than holding a tennis party in the rain?'

'Staying at home, uninvited?' Mother suggested tartly.

Antonia couldn't bear it. 'Perhaps Virginia's only mistake was telling young Stanhope when they were laughing together at the Christmas ball how little she admires the game.'

But it was hopeless. She might as well have tried to shoot a ball back over the net to a champion.

'Virginia is clearly not alone in the business of failing to admire.'

And that was it. Mother had won the match. Up flew Virginia's trembling hands to cover her face, her disappointment and her tears.

And Mother turned to Antonia.

'And what is this I hear from Mrs Fannin about your bruiting your opinions far and wide?'

To give herself a moment to think, Antonia feigned reflection. 'At Sunday School, was that, Mama? Did I mistake something in my lesson for the little ones?'

'I think you understand me well enough, Antonia.'

Antonia steeled herself to gaze, unflinching, into her mother's eyes. Which of her sins would it be? Confessing to Mr Sparrow that she had her doubts about two of the articles in the Holy Creed? Insisting to Miss Hetherington that, on the contrary, blackberries and apples were a very happy mix in pies? Accusing the lads at the ford of horrid cruelty to the frogs they trapped? Or simply offering to Mrs Bethany the housekeeper the opinion that Maria hadn't the strength to carry such heavy coal buckets?

Any. All. None. It made no difference. Clearly, the storm was on its way.

'The apple, of course, never falls far from the tree. You are fully as outspoken as your father! But what is fitting for a man scarcely befits a silly chit of a girl. What are monkeys and orang-utans and Mr Darwin to do with you? And what embarrassment, to have my own daughter correcting her elders and betters!'

So that was it. A cheerful little wrangle about Creation over a stile with Jamie Crawford's mother! How these petty little reports slunk back.

And how they were used.

'You will, of course, take back your books directly.'

Now this was spite indeed. 'Take back my books?'

'All of them. Every last one. And you must tell Mr Sparrow that he is not to lend you any more.'

'But . . .'

'No arguments, Antonia. How can I let you loose in Mr Sparrow's library if I can't depend on your good sense?'

'But all I said to Mrs Crawford was . . .'

'Antonia! It's not your place to bicker. No more books!'

Desperately, Antonia looked around for help. Everything else had been horrid, fair enough. But this was *important*. What was she to do without her books? And this was not going to be the sort of rule that was here today and gone tomorrow. Antonia could tell that. This was like being 'too old to paddle in the lake', or 'forbidden to speak to the Gibsons'. It would stick.

Beside her, little Lucia's hands were wringing in her lap. But of what use was that? Nobody spoke. One by one, Antonia sought their support with pleading eyes. They knew what her books meant. All of their lives, they'd seen her curled up in trees, on window seats, in armchairs, on the bend in the attic stairs, always with a book in her hand. But, one by one, her sisters dropped their gazes safely to the table, leaving her to fight this battle alone.

'But how will I manage? There are so few books here! And Mr Sparrow has so many. He helps me choose, and I know he takes the greatest care not to furnish me with anything he thinks unsuitable. He says so *often*.'

It was like talking to a clear glass wall. Her mother turned away.

'Please, Mother! *Please*!'

'Antonia, be warned. I do dislike scenes at the table.'

A cheap schoolboy trick, to drive a body into a fit of wild misery, then take it to task for its lack of composure.

'This is *not fair*!'

'Each word you utter makes it clear your reading does not so much enrich your young mind as warp it to wilfulness. You'll take every last book straight back to Mr Sparrow within the hour!'

And now the tears of fury and frustration spurted.

Once again, Mrs Cox turned away her face. Was it to hide a look of distaste? Or one of satisfaction? For as this, the last and least fragile of her daughters, finally dissolved into floods, Mrs Cox reached, as if replete at last, for the little silver calling bell.

'Yes, Rosie. Now we're quite finished. You may clear.'

Her heart now as heavy as her bag was light, Antonia strode home through pouring rain, hating her sisters, every last one of them. Despising them utterly. Craven, craven, craven. Hadn't she been the first to spring to poor Hester's defence by begging her mother not to talk any more about horrible Jamieson? Then she'd risked real displeasure by reminding everyone that little Lucia's catastrophe with the rose had led to better things next year. And as for her support of Virginia! Antonia had managed to weave a merry and spirited interchange out of those few stiff words she'd seen exchanged, to no one's satisfaction, at the ball. If she could conjure dignity out of thin air for Virginia, couldn't Virginia speak real truth for her? 'Mother, you know Antonia can't live without her books. Please don't do this to her. *Please* think again.'

And what had they managed between them? Not a word. A few fingers twisting unhappily in a lap, and that was it. But surely sisterhood should work both ways. And if they were content to make no efforts to keep Antonia herself from bookless misery, why should she strain herself for them? So she might, after all, pass on what Mr Sparrow had let drop about young George Stanhope's opinions. Instead of letting the horrid indiscretion distress only herself, now she could share it. It would, at least, explain the long silence from the Grange, and stop her sister lifting her head in foolish hope each time a letter came. After all, as Mother so often said, the apple never falls far from the tree. Outspoken as her father, Antonia's was a nature on which such a secret might weigh heavily . . . Yes, she would tell.

Over the stile she went, and down the cart-track. And there, snagged in wet brambles, was a spot of pink. It was a ribbon rose from one of Lucia's Sunday frocks. How she'd be panicking! On any other day, Antonia would get herself scratched ragged in the determination to tug it free, and carry it home, triumphant. 'See what I found, Lucia, in the hedge? Now run and fetch thread, and Virginia will make it good before Mother even notices.'

This time, Antonia passed it by without a second look. If the full force of Lucia's efforts to bring things right were simple hand-wringing, then let her wring them for herself. Why should Antonia risk her own dress and her mother's wrath, when no one tried to mend things for her?

Through the swing gate, and into the dripping orchard. And it was fitting that, in this dank place, with her dank heart, she found the baby rabbit, torn by fox or stoat, dead on the footpath where soft, haunted Hester would see it on her way to feed the hens. Antonia drew her foot back just in time. Why kick it into long grass? Let it lie! For that was Hester's way, she'd seen that clearly enough over the table. If you can just do nothing, then just do that.

And here they were, coming across the lawns. Strange, to her, how, with her new resolutions, she felt so much more friendly towards them all and – as if quite forgetting the bloody tangle at her feet – drew them all closer. 'Don't go by the cart-track, Lucia. You will spoil your shoes. Come this way, through the orchard. Virginia, I have such tittle-tattle! You'll never guess what Mrs Sparrow overheard George Stanhope say about you! Do come and hear!'

And even stranger, to them, how, as her voice grew stronger, she herself seemed to be slipping further and further away, back down the wet footpath into the shadow of the largest tree.

Partners in Crime

'You're fired!' he shouted at her when she finally came through the door.

'Oh, Ned,' she said, handing him a bag full of vegetables to carry. 'It's only Wednesday.'

'I know it's only Wednesday,' he stormed. 'And this is the third time this week you've taken over two hours for lunch, so you're fired. Hump and Son can't afford to keep you.'

'Hump and Son can't afford *not* to,' she said, and sailed up the stairs.

Ned sighed. She was right. He couldn't fire her. She

was the only secretary in Greater London who could read his father's writing. Weighed down by his worries and her shopping, he fell in behind.

'Marry me, then,' he wailed.

'No,' she said, reaching the landing.

'Why not?' he asked, as he always did.

Laughing, she shut the door to the Ladies in his face.

He trailed disconsolately into the cramped and cluttered office where Edward Hump, curled like a malignant owl over a jumbo-sized pad, was composing his eighteenth whodunnit that year.

'She's getting worse,' Ned told his father. 'She'll have to go.'

'Go away yourself,' said Edward Hump. He was wondering whether, just for a change, he might let the butler be the murderer after all. But then the vicar should have attended Miss Phipps's tea party in chapter two for an alibi, and she had already printed those pages. If he rewrote them now, she would be furious. Feeling art thwarted, he wiped his pen on the curtains she had chosen. It would have to be the vicar, as usual. He promised himself that next time he would work the plot out fully before he began.

Ned was astride the swivel chair now, fiddling with the keys on her word processor, and grumbling softly. 'She's *never* been this bad before.' Irritably he drummed his fingers on the keyboard, and a series of strange and unaccountable letters suddenly appeared on her screen.

Yet another victimpf*q!?!

'Two whole hours and a quarter,' he muttered, freshly outraged. 'For *lunch*.'

He tried to delete his small contribution to his father's work, stopping only when he noticed line after line on the screen rapidly melting away. 'She's been awful since the last time I proposed to her.'

Edward Hump toyed with the notion of a torrid affair between the vicar and Miss Phipps in chapter seven. Sales might rocket, solving Hump and Son's financial problems; but finding the idea rather distasteful, he discarded it again. After all, money wasn't everything.

'When *did* you last propose to her?' he asked his son.

Ned looked at his watch. 'About six minutes ago,' he said. 'But I really meant the time before that.' He took another look at the empty screen. She would be furious. 'I know she'll marry me sooner or later,' he said mournfully. 'I just wish she'd hurry up.' He spread his hands. 'What's *wrong* with me?'

Edward Hump despaired of his son at times, and this was one of them. He placed his pen on the jumbo pad, where it lay, leaking gently.

'Forgive me if I trample,' he began courteously. 'But perhaps she would view your suit with more favour if you were to refrain from thrusting a week's notice in her face with one hand as often as you offer her the other in marriage.'

His son did not look up. He was making a chain from her paper-clips.

'Perhaps there are finer points to your policy of courtship,' Edward Hump kindly suggested. 'But steeped though I am by trade in the machinations of warped minds, they escape me.'

His son was rooting for more clips in the corner of her desk drawer.

'Your bearing strikes me as odd,' pursued Edward Hump. 'Not calculated to engage a young lady's confidence in the long-term prospects for any normal relationship. You take her out to lunch and detain her, proposing, for over two hours. On return, you fire her for being late.' He rescued his pen from the ink flood that threatened to submerge it. 'In her less flighty moments, she may have doubts about you.'

Ned held up his chain of her paper-clips. Although it was nearly a metre long, it did not cheer him appreciably.

'*I* don't take her to lunch,' he said.

'Pardon me,' said his father. 'You used to. I thought

you still did. It seemed to fit nicely. Each day this week, for example, she has risen from her seat promptly at one o'clock, planted a kiss on my cheek and said happily: "Heigh-ho. Off to see Ted." Or Ned. I forget which. But it's all the same thing.'

Ned tore the paper-clip chain to bits in his fury.

'It's not the same thing at all!' he snapped. 'Not at all!'

The next day, at one o'clock, he followed her. She set off at a brisk pace down the High Street. Ned shambled behind, hands sunk into trouser pockets, staring morosely at the back of her long legs. At one point she shot into a chemist's shop. Intrigued by a display of greying trusses in the window, he almost lost her.

Emerging, she jaywalked across the road, and a tanker driver braked to let her pass, whistling appreciatively. Ned jaywalked after her, and the same driver speeded up to cut him off, with a nasty oath.

Loftily, Ned ignored him. The end of the enormous tanker finally rolled clear, and Ned saw her legs disappearing into the museum's revolving door. He hared up the steps, but the foyer was empty.

The museum was vast – three floors with numerous offshoots, two exhibition halls and an outdoor annexe. Ned was not a systematic man. It took him an hour and three-quarters to find her, and it was his third time around.

She was standing in a huge, vaulted chamber, half-hidden by a trio of walruses, stroking the snout of a large stuffed seal. She seemed to be telling it something.

Ned leaned, panting and bemused, against a large elk. He felt a little cheered. Perhaps Ted had stood her up. Perhaps she would marry Ned on the rebound.

A polite cough startled Ned from his pleasant thoughts. A museum attendant was at his side.

'Would you mind?' the attendant said. 'Them elks is precious.'

Ned pointed across to the walruses. 'What about *her*,

then?' he demanded peevishly. 'She's stroking that thing's *nose*.'

'That's different,' the attendant said. 'That seal's been condemned.'

Accepting this explanation, Ned took his own weight.

'Besides,' the attendant went on. 'She's gentle with him. *Leptonychotes weddelli* don't come to no harm from her.'

'Who don't?'

'*Leptonychotes weddelli*.' After a pause he added loftily: 'Weddell's seal to you.'

Knitting his brows, he, like Ned, stared across the room. 'Odd, though. *She* calls him Ted.'

Ned's large mouth fell open.

'Or Ned. One or the other. It's all the same thing.'

'Only to the half-deaf or half stupid,' Ned muttered unpleasantly.

Deeply hurt, the attendant made to go. Ned caught his arm. 'I'm terribly sorry, truly I am,' he pleaded. 'I'm a little overwrought.'

Mollified as much by Ned's obvious misery as by the apology, the attendant once again became expansive. 'Comes here every day,' he said. 'Strokes that there seal's nose and talks to him for hours. Even brings sandwiches sometimes.'

'For the seal?' asked Ned, astonished.

'For her lunch,' the attendant said, eyeing Ned narrowly. 'The seal is dead.' He rocked proprietorially on his heels. 'Strange that she should choose him from all this lot.' He made a generous gesture which took in all his finer specimens, himself and Ned.

'Very,' Ned muttered bitterly.

'And downright unsanitary, when you come to think. That seal must be fifty years old if he's a day. Stuffing's *pouring* out. That's why he's been condemned. Only yesterday I told her, "You ought to choose someone else to talk to, dear. How about a nice moose," I said. But she wouldn't have it. Oh, no. Women are like that, though.' He scratched his chin. 'Said he reminds her of someone she loves.'

Ned went all cunning.

'Did you ask her why she hasn't married this man who looks like a seal and whom she loves?' he asked, casual to a degree.

'No,' said the attendant, and wandered off to prise a small child from the knees of his nice moose.

Ned glared, dispirited, at the elk against whom he had been forbidden to lean. The elk glared back, looking a bit like she did when she was in one of her moods. Finding the odds against him intoxicating, Ned tried to stare the elk out. The elk won, and Ned looked round again.

She had gone.

He approached the seal warily, from the rear. Horny hind flippers led up into threadbare fur, mottled cream and fawn, and blotching into silver on the back of its head. The taxidermist's seam spiralled from one end of the seal to the other, like a stocking gone awry. The seal smelled of mould and mothballs, shed stuffing in places, and had no neck. And it reminded her of someone she loved? Ned was not a vain man, but it crossed even his mind that to kindle a love so unflattering might perhaps be worse than kindling no love at all. He poked the seal's paunch experimentally, and a whiff of decaying fur rose up and hit him full in the face. Ned decided that there must be another man in her life, not noted for personal freshness, and by name of Ted. He walked round to the front of the seal to inspect the stuffed facial likeness of his rival for her hand.

It was only then that he saw the seal's eyes. They loomed up at him, set wide above bristled cheeks, large and chocolate brown, and a little bloodshot around the edges. Ned stared at them, appalled. He had seen both of them before. They were his eyes too. There was no possibility of his being mistaken. He recognised them from shaving.

Panicking, Ned looked away.

The elk had brown eyes, too. He supposed, thinking about it, that most animals did. Feeling calmed by this reflection he looked back at the seal. His shock was again immediate. No other animal had eyes like these eyes, and these eyes were like his. This seal's eyes brimmed with memories so forlorn, the cool elk and his brothers could not guess at them. Ned found these eyes worse than harrowing. They told of all the pitiful hours this seal had passed, vigilant and alone, on drifting ice flows, longing for better days. The bleak Antarctic twilight had brought this seal to such desperation that he had lumbered off towards his very hunters, prepared to hazard life itself for the sound of a muffled voice, or the sight of two eyes that were not his own, gazing back reproachfully from an ice looking-glass.

Ned swallowed, near to tears. He stretched out his hand, as she had done, to comfort the seal with a caress. But he could not bring himself to touch it. It would, he thought, be like saying 'There, there' to a shipwreck.

Ned began walking round and round the seal, thinking. Could it be that he looked like that (give or take a few whiskers) to her? Could it be that she felt this shattered each time he turned his own eyes on her, imploring marriage? Then small wonder that she always refused. No one could live with that seal, and stay sane. Why should she take such a risk with him? There was no hope.

Ned stopped circling the seal, and began walking up and down the chamber in straight lines.

Of course there was hope. The seal was stuffed, and must always look as it did now; whereas Ned was alive, and could possibly look different on occasions. He was not forever shaving or proposing, after all.

Ned wandered off to the sides of the chamber in search of his own reflection. Stationing himself four-square before the dark furry tummy of a conveniently encased bat, Ned stared at himself in the glass. His own eyes looked, if that were possible, a shade more woebegone even than the seal's. Ned gulped and began his experiment.

He smiled at himself warmly, unconscious of the attendant's curious stare. The face crumpled up, as smiling faces do; but the eyes remained tragic – two islands of suffering in a sea of good cheer.

He tried a knowing, man-to-man look. The eyebrows played their part with enthusiasm, but the eyes refused to be drawn.

He told himself a short joke, and chuckled at the punch line. The eyes were unamused.

Sympathetic understanding and swashbuckling arrogance fared no better. Ned made one last attempt – a depraved leer. The bat seemed quite taken, but the eyes were indifferent. Ned lost his temper.

The eyes lit up, transformed. Ned hardly recognised himself. He sighed with relief, unguardedly, and the eyes wavered. So he thought of how she made him carry her vegetables all the way up the stairs, and then slammed doors in his face. The eyes rallied. He recalled the sneaky way in which his father had for years postponed all increases in his salary. The eyes became positively frenzied.

A rare feeling of exhilaration swept through Ned as he stood, seemingly riveted to the bat's tummy, remembering one affront to his pride after another, and watching his eyes flash. The attendant, lurking behind the walruses, thought it was odd, the sort of creatures people took fancies to, nowadays. He wondered momentarily if the bat reminded Ned of someone he loved.

Ned, taking one last look in the bat, thought it was astonishing just how much he had brooked from them both. He strode from the museum, a new man.

The slamming of the office door caused Edward Hump to catch his funny bone on the *Dictionary of Acids and Poisons*. A large blot of ink fell from his pen on to the inspector's explanation of the fiendish way in which the vicar, with the help of Miss Phipps, had disposed of all nine bodies overnight.

'You're back, then,' he said, testing the small ink pool for depth with the tip of his finger. 'Would you be so good as to pass me some blotting paper?'

In answer, Ned swung the door open once more, and slammed it shut with even more force than before. Edward Hump looked up.

So did she. Indeed, she went further. She stopped typing and, pushing the keyboard forward a little way, rested her elbows comfortably on the desk, and her dimpled chin on her cupped palms.

He waved a banker's order threateningly in her direction.

'How much does a normal person earn?' he demanded of her. 'Someone normal, my age, like me. How much?'

She told him. His eyebrows shot up in astonishment.

He glared venomously at his father. Then he snatched up a pen from the marmalade pot full of them on her desk, and filled the amount in on the order. 'I'm not earning a penny less than a normal person any longer,' he muttered fiercely.

He slammed the order down in front of Edward Hump.

'Go on, then,' he said aggressively. 'Sign it.'

Edward Hump peered with interest at the amount Ned had decided to earn.

'I can't pay you that much,' he said. 'It's as much as I earn myself.'

'That's quite all right,' Ned told him. 'You're retiring at the end of this month.'

He pulled his father's resignation from a trouser pocket and uncrumpled that, too, upon Edward Hump's desk.

'Go on, then,' he repeated. 'Sign them both.'

Edward Hump wished his son would go away.

He wanted to get the vicar defrocked and safely imprisoned by the weekend, so that he could get on with some gardening. Laboriously, he stained a dotted line at the foot of the banker's order with his spidery runes.

With unaccustomed adroitness, Ned whisked the precious slip of paper away and pocketed it. 'Now the other,' he said firmly.

Edward Hump turned his flagging attention to the other foreign body on his desk, and made a big effort.

'Much as the notion of resignation from Hump and Son appeals,' he began, 'and, Lord knows, the shrubbery could do with some sustained attention . . .'

'Blast the shrubbery!' shouted Ned. 'Sign it!'

Edward Hump made a little scratchy mess on the spot his son's finger indicated. Almost immediately, another drawback struck him. He nodded in the direction of the only secretary in Greater London who could read his writing.

'What about her?' he said. 'If I retire, it's curtains for her. She'll have to go. There'll be no work for her. Possibly she'll starve.'

'She won't starve,' said Ned.

'She may well,' his father disagreed. 'Her filing is dismal. No one else would employ her.'

'*I'm* going to employ her,' said Ned. 'I'll feed her. I'll feed her lots of milk. We'll be needing another "and Son". Or "and Daughter". She can have them. She can have lots. Overflowing cotfuls.'

'I see,' said Edward Hump. 'It's all clear to me now. You're planning on altering the tone of the books we produce. Hump and Son is moving from murder into romance.' He waggled a finger at the two of them. 'I warn you, the outcome is generally much the same.'

'We'll be all right,' Ned said, turning to his beloved. 'Won't we?'

She turned on him that cool, elk-like look that drove him wild. 'Will we?' she said. 'Oh, will we really? And suppose I don't choose to have your mangy babies, Ned Hump?'

'I warned you,' Edward Hump muttered. 'Romance is dead.'

But Ned didn't hear him. He was beside himself with rage.

'Choose? *Choose*?' He was shouting to make the light bulbs tremble. 'You're going to choose. You're going to choose right *now*. You're going to choose between that disgusting old mothbag seal in that crumbling museum, and that malevolent old mothbag, my father, in that ink-swamped desk over there, and this fine strapping person, myself, standing before you. And you are going to choose *me*!'

He thrust his face, scarlet with rage, over the word processor at her, and they glared at each other.

Suddenly she smiled, and kissed him wetly on the nose.

A few days later, while his father was engaging the registrar in a bit of light chat about one of his earlier masterpieces, *The Bride in the Bathtub*, Ned Hump signed his name with a flourish wherever his new wife placed her dainty, freshly manicured finger.

'There,' she said, pointing. 'And there and there and there and there.'

It seemed an awful lot of places to have to sign your name, just to get married. And his father, appending his name as witness whilst explaining to the registrar how best to chop up a body, said much the same.

Then the three of them ambled happily through the doors into the sunlight, arm in arm, and as the photographer stepped forward to greet them, Ned Hump honoured his bride with his first sweet nothing.

'*Now* you're fired,' he whispered in her ear.

She smiled imperturbably. Pulling a slim roll of legal papers out of her bouquet of lilies, she lifted her face for her first married kiss.

'Don't be so silly, Ned,' she said to him sweetly as the photographer took his first picture. 'You've only just this minute made me a partner.'

Poor, Poor Cordelia

The house I live in is a hundred years old, built on another far, far older. Upon the gates, intricately wrought into rusting iron, there is a sundial. On its face . . .

Aldwyn lifted an eyebrow at PC Angel, who was pouring the tea.

'That's it, sir,' Angel said. 'Honest. The lad wrote it out himself down in the cells, while we were snowed up. Out it all came, every word, and we never so much as nudged him, sir.'

'Fancy.' Aldwyn prised off his wet shoes and, turning over a couple of sheets, read the first line to catch his eye: *I'd leave the garden with all its hidden places and moving shadows . . .*

'What does the boy think?' Aldwyn demanded of Angel. 'That we can't afford my bus fare to the scene of the crime?'

'I think he was in a bit of a state, like, with all those sundials and rusty gates and things,' Angel said kindly. 'But I must say, I thoroughly enjoyed it myself. There's nothing like a nice read. Now you've traipsed through all this nasty weather to get here, why don't you settle down with a strong cup of tea and have a good read? You'll feel much better.'

In honour of the occasion, he turned the gas fire up from miser-rate to low.

Aldwyn didn't lift his eyes from the pile of white pages that had already absorbed him, but he stretched out an unconscious hand for the teacup.

'Thanks, Angel,' he said absently.

The house I live in is a hundred years old, built on another far, far older. Upon the gates, intricately wrought into rusting iron, there is a sundial. On its face, Death is engraved, eyeless and grinning, with leatherish skin falling in tatters about his bones. He holds a pale, amazed girl by the hand, and the inscription reads: *Now Rest In Peace.*

When I was younger, I spent a lot of time beneath that sundial. I'd leave the garden with all its hidden places and moving shadows and, climbing the high stone wall, I'd lower myself until the toe holds on the sundial's weathered face would let me drop safely on to the wide lawns that slope as far down as the dark of the forest. I'd hear my baby sister Josie howl for the sudden loss of me, and then my mother's voice, reproving, comforting. As quiet settled on the garden again, I'd lie back in the sunlight on the grass and watch the clouds roll by, over the sundial and myself.

I made several sketches of the girl on the sundial. If

that sounds odd to you, I should point out it's not so easy finding real sitters round here. Before I went off to art school in London, I'd probably painted twenty dogs and cats and tortoises for every real, live, patient person. If Josie was at her friends' houses, or at school, the girl on the sundial was frequently my only resource. I started drawings of her so often that I had cupboards full of them. And all gone wrong. In every one, some aspect of grinning Death himself, some hint of his own dusty bones and withered folds of skin overshadowed my sketch, as if the girl whose hand, rigid with terror, he clasped in his own had somehow already been mortally infected.

So Josie was a far better prospect and, each chance I had, I painted her. I have drawings of my sister from the cradle. Now she's nine. And that's why, when I came home from London for Christmas and my mother told me about Cordelia, I felt so uneasy. Nine years old is a little late to make up an imaginary friend.

'Cordelia?'

'Yes. Just Cordelia. And if you ask Josie what her other name is, she simply goes blank.'

'Where's this Cordelia supposed to live?'

'Somewhere round here. Nowhere particular.'

'How old is she?'

My mother, I thought, paled a little before answering: 'Hundreds of years.'

'Oh, really!'

I burst out laughing. But something in my mother's face made me break off and ask one more question.

'Does Josie admit that this Cordelia is a fantasy?'

My mother didn't answer that.

'Oh, Tom,' she said. 'Do what you can!'

During the next few days, I spent as much time as I could alone with my sister. On our long walks I tried encouraging her to talk about all the things in her life I could think of: schoolwork, home, hobbies – but most of all, friends. I kept returning to this topic like a moth to a candle. And as the days went by I heard more than I care to remember about Tracy and Clare and Simon and Surina. Cordelia's name, though, never came up.

In the end, I asked Josie outright: 'Who is Cordelia?'

'A girl.'

'You haven't mentioned her. Is she a friend of yours?'

'Not really.'

'No?'

Uneasy, she looked down and scuffed her shoes together.

'Maybe. A bit.'

'Who *is* Cordelia?' And, when the silence grew uncomfortable: 'What does she look like?'

Josie looked relieved. It seemed this question was far easier to answer.

'She looks just like the girl on the sundial.'

Flippantly, I said: 'I hope Death isn't after her, as well.'

'No,' Josie said gravely. 'He was, once. But now she

thinks that he's forgotten her.'

'I see,' I said, though clearly I didn't. But I remembered what my sister had told my mother, and so I asked: 'And is she really hundreds of years old?'

'Yes,' Josie said. 'Yes, she is. Poor thing. Poor thing . . .'

I stared at her. The tears were flooding from my sister's eyes.

'Poor thing,' she said again, her voice choked. 'Poor, poor Cordelia.'

Shaking, I took her home as fast as I could.

I told my parents I was absolutely sure that there was nothing to worry about; it was simply a stage; it would pass over. My parents said as glibly back that they were quite sure I was right; they'd wait and see; early days yet. My mother, I could tell, was close to tears.

And, slowly, the last days before Christmas went by. Now Josie never spoke of Cordelia, but since she so clearly still believed in her, it was as if the wretched girl was with us all the time. We were all troubled – all but

Josie – with growing feelings of unease.

On Christmas Eve my parents set off, on foot, to share a seasonal drink with neighbours. They left me in charge of the house and my sister. I shut the door against the bitter rain that was just turning into sleet, but before I even had time to swing around, Josie had rushed from the living-room into my arms.

'Tom! Tom!' she tugged my sleeve. 'Cordelia's here. She's in there, by the fire, waiting for you.'

'Come in the kitchen,' I said. 'I'll make you lemonade.'

'*No*, Tom! Come *in*. She's *waiting* for you. Cordelia's been *waiting*.'

'How long?' I scoffed. 'Hundreds of years?'

(I hadn't realised quite what anxiety I felt until it turned like that, so fast, into anger.)

Josie was shocked. 'Tom!'

I strode into the room in a fury. I was so sure, so entirely convinced, that I yelled at Josie: 'See! No one's here!' even before I saw Cordelia hunched on the rug beside the fire, wrapped in the rainbow-coloured coverlet pulled from the sofa.

Slowly she turned to look at me. The light from Christmas candles on the mantelpiece swept right across her perfect face – that face I knew so well and tried to draw so many times when I was younger. The look she had upon the sundial was different, certainly: the girl that Death held firmly by the hand was harder, ugly from sudden fright. This was a grave and tranquil child that I was seeing now, a child half absorbed in firelight, half curious to see the newcomer. But it was clearly the same face.

'Cordelia . . .'

She smiled at me. I dropped into my father's chair and stared at her, confused, appalled. Josie moved to the fire's edge and sat contentedly beside her friend. Each time Cordelia turned her head to smile at me, candlelight flickered on her cheekbones and made her look as strangely sick and deathly haggard as I remembered all my old drawings of her ended up looking before, frustrated out of mind, I tossed them out of sight inside a drawer. Then, suddenly, she'd seem a child again, her flesh as pink and round as Josie's, her eyes almost as trouble-free.

'Cordelia . . .'

But there was nothing I could think to say. You can't tell someone you can see that you don't believe they are there, for there they are. Cordelia sat on our hearthrug, picking at threads and tracing patterns with her fingertips. Josie rocked back and forth beside the fire. I think back now and see it as a very peaceful waiting time. Cordelia was waiting for me.

We sat a very long time before I dared reach out to touch her. The sound of sleet driving relentlessly against the windowpanes was all we heard until Cordelia began to sing in a small voice a strange and unfamiliar song, one steeped in misery and longing, with old, old words:

'This ae night,
This ae night,
At my hearth rallie
Sleet, fire and friend and candlelight.
May Heaven receive
My soul.'

I stretched out my hand to touch her hair. The soft brown shine of it felt matted and brittle beneath my fingers. I ran my hand down the side of her cheek. The skin that looked so pink and warm was dry and withered. Her throat, where it was golden in the firelight, was shrivelled and horrid to the touch. A stench, the sour, tainted stink of decay, rose in my face, sickening me. I drew my hand away in terror, but when I dared to look again, it was as if my own imaginings had overcome me momentarily. For Cordelia sat, as young and fresh and serene on the rug as when I first caught sight of her. But she still sang, under her breath, her forlorn, ancient song of longing for death and peace and oblivion, and turned on me a look of such need that, when I realised I had understood the endless, living horror of her situation, I could not deny her. I could not be as cruel as that.

'Get up, Cordelia,' I said. 'Get *up*.'

I did not wait for her to hesitate. I took hold of her arm and forced her to rise. The smell of putrefaction rose again. Cordelia's wrist felt nothing but sinew and bone beneath my fingers, but I held tight. I pulled her after me, across the room, and all the while my sister kept her eyes on the fire's colours, still rocking peaceably, for all the world as if she hadn't seen or heard a thing.

I half led, half dragged Cordelia along the hall. Catching a blurred reflection of her face in a glass pane, I turned my head aside before I saw if the warped, purplish image there was just the drop-mottling of sleet behind, or the true, hideous face of the fast-shrivelling thing I pulled, unresisting, with me into wet darkness.

The sleet was blinding. Dragging this living corpse across the grass I stumbled and, clutching the wrist in my hand more tightly, felt all my fingernails shred through the withered paper of its skin, and touch the bone beneath. I was too filled with horror and decision to loosen my grip. I hauled the ghastly thing after me, down, down the garden, until the wrought-iron gates were visible at last through the wet sheen of driving sleet, and I could see that for the first time ever to my memory, the rusting chains hung free, and the gates were ajar.

I forced the bundle through. I pinned the raddled, sexless dwarf up on the gates, hung that foul bag of loosening bones spilling from the coverlet up on a curlicue of black iron. And only when it was hanging there, in eerie, shifting light under the shadow of Death on the sundial, did I let go.

The thing jerked and swayed spasmodically, the shrivelled crone's face grey and glistening with globs of sleet. Its stench swarmed over me.

'I'll do what I can!' I screamed over the wind.

The scraggy, wasted creature twisted with rage and fear, prune-ugly, livid, painful to watch.

I shut my eyes and slid my hands round its throat, and strangled it. It took a long while. It took all my strength and courage and decision, and all my kindness, too, to strangle poor, poor Cordelia. It took so long that when I finally opened my eyes, I was so cold I, too, slid down against the black iron of the gate, as if the glitter of the snow underfoot could be warmth or peace. I took the rainbow coverlet from where it lay, in a small heap on the ground, and sat wrapped in it, keeping vigil. The sickly, putrid smell had cleared away, and I could breathe again.

I looked above me, up at the sundial, huge and shot-silver.

'Now rest in peace, Cordelia,' I whispered, comforting myself and her.

An echo from her song came back to me.

'May Heaven receive my soul.'

'Now rest in peace.'

Aldwyn laid down the last page with a shiver. He looked up at PC Angel, standing waiting, idly picking at loose threads in his uniform.

'This lad. Is he . . . ?'

'Bats, sir? No, not a bit of it. The doctor's seen him. Sane as we are, so it seems. Bit moody, mind, but that's to be expected, down in those cells. No place to spend your Christmas Day snowed up, is it?'

'Who brought him in?'

'MacDonald, sir. Came on him suddenly, thrashing about in a snowdrift, babbling about strangling little Cordelia. He knows you don't like people in over holidays, sir. But he said he thought he ought, considering . . .'

'No body, I suppose?' Aldwyn asked, a shade

wistfully.

'MacDonald had a good look, naturally. But all he found was some old bones. He says they might be human bones, they might be animal bones. But, either way, this lad can't be responsible. They're far too old. MacDonald thinks that when the gates were forced apart, these bones were sort of scraped up out of the earth.'

'And what about Cordelia?'

'Nothing there, sir. No one who lives close seems to recognise the name. The lad's mother said . . .' and Angel rooted through the notes: ' "There's no one round here called Cordelia and never has been." MacDonald says she was quite fierce about it.'

'And the lad's sister. What did she say?'

'She said: "Not any more".'

'Not any more?'

'Yes, sir. It's down here in MacDonald's notes. "Not any more".'

The two men looked at one another uneasily for a short moment. Then Aldwyn pulled himself together.

'Right, then,' he said. 'You'd better give the lad a lift home as soon as that road's snowploughed clear again. No crime, after all.' The disappointment made him irritable. 'No body, no missing child, no evidence of foul play. No crime.' He threw the sheaf of papers down on the desk. 'Why didn't you tell me all this before?'

'I didn't want to spoil the story for you,' soothed PC Angel. 'I always hate it when people tell *me* the end.'

Aldwyn picked up the teapot.

'I suppose there are dafter ways of spending Christmas Day in the cells,' he said. And, tipping the teapot, he poured steadily. The tea spilled on the pile of papers. It soaked quickly through the flimsy sheets. The ink blurred and swam unrecognisably into a large, blue, sopping puddle. Aldwyn kept pouring till the tea leaves came out, and the confession was unreadable.

The Ship of Theseus

'Careers advice!' Mr Lang's lip curled. 'I'll give you careers advice! Find out what you like doing most in all the world, and then look for someone who'll pay you to do it.' And I thought how, by that way of judging, my dad's in the right job. He's a philosopher. I couldn't even say the word when I was little. It came out as 'flossifer' and I hadn't the faintest idea what it meant, except I assumed it had something to do with that peculiar white stringy stuff they kept next to the toothpaste.

Not that he didn't keep trying to explain. 'I *think*,' he said. 'That's what I do for a living. *Think*.'

Mum's got no time for it. *'Thinking*, you call it? *Arguing*, more like,' she always corrects him, if she's listening. Because he doesn't seem to do it very quietly. He's always thumping away about one thing or another, hoping that someone will pitch in and tell him he's wrong, so he can put them right about how he isn't. I'm like Mum. I act deaf – and stupid, too, if necessary – to get out of it. But Tabby listens.

Maybe she should be a philosopher too.

Strange thought. Because they're really weird, the things that it's his job to think about. Like when Tabs was little and splashing round in the bathtub while Dad was shaving, and she asked him suddenly, out of the blue: 'How do I know that all this round me isn't just a dream?'

He spun round so fast, so thrilled, he nicked himself quite badly. 'Look at her!' he called to Mum, blotting the blood from his chin. 'The philosopher's daughter! Four years old, and already an ontological sceptic!'

Whatever that is. And I must say, it does seem Tabby's far more on his wavelength than I am. I am forever walking into rooms to find the two of them wrangling away. Sometimes it's just normal family stuff, like her going on at him about finally finding the time to dismantle her stupid Squirrel's Night-time Hidey-hole halfway up the wall, so Mum can move in her new proper bed. (She is nearly *eleven*.) Or him grinding on about why tonight can't be the night they sleep under the stars. (She's been desperate to do this ever since I lent her *Oriole of the Outback*.) But Mum says she can only sleep outside if Dad is with her.

And he never gets round to it.

Too busy thinking.

This morning, it wasn't the bunk bed or the sleep-out. It was The Ship of Theseus.

Dad was explaining. 'So Theseus has this great big wooden ship, and everyone calls it The Ship of Theseus.'

'Makes sense,' I said. (I like to stick my oar in when

I can – which isn't often.)

'And it gets more and more battered as time goes by – all his long voyages. So gradually, one by one, over the years, each single plank gets replaced. Every last one. And – this is the good bit – all the old planks just happen to float away in the very same direction, and fetch up, one by one, on the very same island.'

'Oh, very likely,' I scoffed. But Tabs was listening really hard.

'Now,' Dad said. 'On this island, it just so happens there's a master ship-builder, marooned for years. So he collects all the planks as they wash up on his beach, and one day, when he thinks he's got enough, sets to and builds himself a ship. And it so happens – pure coincidence, you understand – that every single rotting plank ends up in exactly its own place.'

He's grinning at Tabs now, and she's staring back, wide-eyed. It's obvious she can see something that I can't.

'*So*?' I say irritably.

Dad turns to me. 'What do you mean, "*So*?" It's only, put in a nutshell, one of the Great Central Questions of Western Philosophy!'

'What is?'

He stares at me as if I'm practically a halfwit. 'The *problem*, Perdita, is which is The Ship of Theseus?'

'Which?'

'Yes,' he says, trying to be patient. 'Is it the *old* one – I mean the one that's just been rebuilt from all the old planks? Or the new one that Theseus is sailing about in?'

I have to say, I take Mum's line on things like this. 'What does it matter?'

'What does it *matter*? Oh, it's only The Problem of Identity, isn't it?' He's clutching his hair now. 'Sweet heavens! It's only that awesome, overpowering question that's bothered some great philosophers their whole lives long: in what, exactly, is identity invested?' He's practically reeling round the room in his anguish.

Till he sees the look on Tabby's face.

She isn't even listening any more. She's lost in thought. Totally absorbed. Honestly, you'd think, to look at her, she could be Theseus on his firm new deck in a good wind, seeing, to his astonishment, a ship sail past, and wondering: 'Well, which one's mine? Neither? Both? This one? That one? But *why*? Perhaps that one first but, at a certain point, this one – or the other way round. But at which point? And why? Why? *Why*?'

The Philosopher's Daughter! So you can see why I spend so much of my Saturday out in the garden with Mum. We think that they're both daft. By coffee time, they were arguing about whether, if no one ever gets to see a particular tree in the middle of a forest, there's any way of being confident it's there at all. Then, later, as Tabs was setting the table for lunch, they reverted to the business of the sleep-out.

'Well why can't we do it *tonight*?'

'Not tonight, Tabitha. I have a lot of work to get through tomorrow. I'll need a clear head and a good night's sleep.'

'You're always saying that.'

'It's always true.'

Mum poked at the risotto. 'Oh, not the sleep-out argument. Not again, *please*.'

(No point my offering to be with Tabs. All Mum ever says is 'Better one daughter murdered than two.' And even Dad daren't argue.)

Tabby moved back to the bed business. 'Well, why can't Dad at least take down my Squirrel Hidey-hole, so I can get my new bed in?'

'It's not as easy as it looks,' Dad said. 'That little bunk bed of yours is a complicated structure. It'll take time to dismantle it.'

Tabs slammed the last of the knives and forks and spoons down in their places. 'Bed? I'm so big now, it's practically a *cage*.'

'I'd take it down for you,' I offered, to try to help her make Dad feel guilty. 'Except that you've had to sleep in it so long that some of the screw heads are so badly rusted I can't get them started.'

'Don't think I haven't wasted hours of my own life trying,' Mum said, to pile it on.

'All right!' said Dad. 'I give in! Straight after lunch I'll loosen the screws enough for Perds and Tabs to take the thing down.'

'Hurrah!' said Mum. 'At last! And now could you two switch to arguing about something entirely different – especially not the sleep-out.'

I was only away for a moment, fetching the salad bowl. But when I came back, they were already launched. 'Now look, Tabs.' Dad was saying irritably. 'Do try and pay attention. It's quite simple.' Grabbing the knives and forks and spoons she'd only just set in place, he built a sort of track across the table, and then divided it at the end. 'There. See the fork?'

'Which fork?' Tabs asked him.

Dad stabbed the place where his line of knives and forks and spoons split into separate directions. 'This fork here.'

Tabs told him, baffled, 'That's a *spoon*.'

(Honestly, sometimes I reckon, when people think too hard, all the blood must rush away to warm up the clever bits and not leave enough to keep the basics – that's just common sense – working at all. Mum says that's why these really clever people are always hours late, or wandering around lost, or striding about with their woollies unravelling behind them.)

'What he means is the fork in his road,' I explained. 'Not a *fork* fork.'

Now Tabs was ratty. 'Well, he should have *said*.'

Dad was outraged. 'I did say! I explained right at the start. "This is the problem of The Angels at The Fork".'

'We're supposed to be eating with those,' I reminded them.

But, of course, neither of them was even listening. Sometimes you'd never think that Dad was thirty-seven and Tabs was eleven. You'd think they were both *three*, and busy squabbling in some sandpit.

'Ready to go on?' Dad asked Tabs, all sarcastically. 'Well, there are two angels standing by this fork. They look exactly the same. So do the roads. But one leads off to heaven, and the other to hell. And, though the angels are identical, one always tells the truth, and one always lies.'

'Always?'

'Always.' He beamed. 'And you, of course, want to get to heaven. But you can only ask one question. And all an angel can reply is "yes", or "no".'

'That's all?'

'That's all.' He spreads his hands in triumph. 'So, Tabitha, which question should you ask?'

He sat back, waiting. I would have said, 'You obviously know the answer. So you tell me.' But Tabs loves problems like these. Her forehead wrinkles up. Sometimes her fingers twitch as if she's working things through like a maths sum. Sometimes she stares into space. And sometimes she even mutters. I reckon if you saw her on a bus, thinking one through, you might easily reckon she was batty.

Even wrinkling and twitching and muttering didn't help her this time. It really stumped her, you could tell. She was still thinking about it even after Mum served up, and while she ate, and even while we washed up and Dad went to fetch the screwdriver and the oil to loosen the screws on her stupid little bunk bed.

She was still thinking as Dad pulled out the first screw. 'I could ask . . .' She broke off, shaking her head. 'No, that wouldn't work.'

'What?' I asked, holding the end up for Dad as he unscrewed the next bit.

'Well, I could ask . . .' Again she stopped, just as I handed her the next strut. 'No, I couldn't. Because I might be talking to the angel who lies.'

'Couldn't ask what?'

She didn't hear me. She was miles away. She didn't even notice each time I handed her a piece of the bunk bed to put on the heap in the corner by the door. And Dad was so taken up with the excitement of whether or not she'd get it right that he didn't notice he hadn't stopped working. He just kept handing me parts of the bunk bed, then got on with unscrewing the next bit.

Finally he couldn't bear it any longer.

'Give up?'

Neither could she.

'Yes. Give up.'

So, while I was stacking all the pieces of wood to take down to the bottom of the garden, he told her. 'You choose an angel, point up either of the roads, and ask the question: "If I were to ask the other angel if this is the road to heaven, would he say "Yes"?'

She thought about it. You could actually see her

working her way through it. And then her face cleared and she beamed the same way he does. 'Brilliant! Excellent! That is so clever!'

I didn't mean to say it. It just popped out.

'I don't get it.'

Dad shook his head at me. 'That's because you're not *thinking*.'

Tabs turned to explain. 'You see, if the angel's answer is "no", then the road you're pointing along has to be the road to heaven. And if the angel answers "yes", it's the road to hell.'

'But how do you *know*?'

'It's obvious,' said Dad. 'It stands to reason, when you come to *think*.'

Tabby was kinder. 'Look,' she explained as we carried the bits of bunk bed down the garden path to stack them out of the way behind the apple-tree. 'Suppose you just happened to ask the honest angel. She'd truthfully tell you the other angel was going to lie, so "yes" would mean "no" and "no" would mean "yes".'

I managed to think that bit through, though my brain was practically *aching*.

Then, 'Go on,' I said.

'And,' she said, her eyes gleaming just like Dad's, 'if you had happened to ask the angel who tells lies, then she'd have definitely made out that the other would have given you the wrong answer.'

'Ye-es,' I said, still trying to catch up.

'So, just like before, "yes" would have meant "no", and "no" would have meant "yes",' she said triumphantly.

'Aren't angels *he*?' I asked, trying to keep my end up. But she'd dumped her last armful, and set off back to the house. So I just stood there a while, thinking about it.

And then I thought some more.

And that's how it turned out that, when Dad got exasperated with all the noise ('Tabs with her music on far too loud, and you with all that mysterious banging in the garden – you're driving me crazy. Please, can't the two of you just go off to your beds and read quietly or something?') we were as good as gold.

We came back twenty minutes later, ready for bed.

'Goodnight, Dad.'

'Goodnight, Perdita.'

'Night, Dad.'

'Goodnight, Tabs.'

She waited in the doorway, grinning. 'Well? Aren't you coming?'

He looked up, mystified. 'Coming where?'

'Down the garden for the sleep-out.' She spreads her hands, innocent as an angel at a fork. 'You know Mum says I'm not allowed to sleep out without you.'

'But we're not doing that tonight.'

'You suggested it. You only just said, can't we go off to our beds?'

His voice was heartfelt. 'Yes, indeed I did!'

'Right then,' she said. 'I'm only doing what you said. And my bed's outside.'

'Nonsense. I saw your mother and the two of you pushing it into your room.'

'No, no.' She winked at me – the genius who made all this possible, standing there inspecting the blisters on my thumbs. 'Perdita's put my Squirrel's Night-time Hidey-hole together again halfway up the apple-tree – every last plank in the same place. So, just like The Ship of Theseus, it's . . .'

She turned to me. After all, I'd done the work. I ought to be the one to crow it. 'Ta-*ra*! The Bed of Tabitha!'

Be fair. He knows when he's beaten, fair and square. He just trailed up to fetch his blankets and a candle or two, so he could keep working. In fact, I think he was delighted, really. Chuffed to bits.

There's more than one way of being a philosopher's daughter . . .